Forbidden Ties

Ruby Clarke

Contents

Chapter 1

G etting to their house I was completely stunned, it was huge and beautiful. We got down from the car, I didn't pack much, just a box and my backpack. I was led into the house. The living room was large with a bookshelf against the side of the wall, it was filled with books, the dinning area was demarcated by pillars and it was two steps higher than the living room floor.

The woman led me upstairs and we walked past two doors, both on the sides and got to a door on the left hand side. There was another door facing it on the right. The woman I have come to know as Mrs Fidelia opened the door on the left for me, when I entered, I paused to look at it and it was beautiful, an average size teenage girl bedroom, decorated in mostly pink, I didn't really have a favorite color but I did like light blue, I liked pink too anyway.

" Do you like it?" Mrs Fidelia asked bringing me out of my thoughts. I looked at her and nodded with a smile. She seemed so nice, I had alot of questions to asked but decided to settle in first." I'm glad you like it" she smiled back " Go ahead and have a rest, my kids are not home yet, I'm sure they'll love to meet you" she said.

' Kids, She had children? Oh no no no, wait! Did I think she would be childless?' I thought, I was only scared, I didn't want new people like my step siblings, but well, what can I do, I had no choice, I had cousins, I tried to relax myself. I smiled at Mrs Fidelia.

"I'll come get you once it's time for dinner okay?" She said before leaving.

I sighed once she left and stepped further into the room that was now mine and immediately began to arrange my properties.

Later that evening, I had gone downstairs for dinner. Mrs Fidelia and her husband Mr Noah had two sons.

The dinning had six chairs, two on each sides, one at the heads each. Mr Noah sat at the head, Mrs Fidelia sat by him on his right, and I sat by her. The younger son who looked like he was 12 years old, he looked fat, his cheeks were a bit chubby, he had dark brown hair, he sat by Mr Noah on the left, and in front of me was the eldest son, he looked 18, his hair was brown but way lighter than that of the younger son.

He was slim and muscular, not overly muscular, he was very handsome. He had blue eyes, just like Mrs Fidelia's, his nose was firm and well shaped, his lips were pink and plump, not too plump though, his hair fell to the side of his face almost covering one of his eye.

Wait! Have I been starring at him? No one had started eating yet and it felt awkward.

Mr Noah cleared his throat " So... She would be living with us from now on, her name is... Liela, she's your cousin" Mr Noah spoke. "Yes dears" Mrs Fidelia added with a big smile as she looked at me then points towards her Chubby son, "His name is Abel" she stated then nudged towards the very handsome one in front of me " He's Gabriel" she seemed really happy.

" I'm sure you'll all get along well" she added " How come she's our cousin and we're only getting to know her?" Abel asked" It doesn't matter Abel, just treat her like your sister" Mr Noah spoke" But how can I treat her like my sister when I've never had a sister before?" Abel asked again" Stop asking questions Abel" Mrs Fidelia warned him." How old is she?" Abel asked again

"I'm 16" I said and everyone went silent, making me regret speaking. I looked at Gabriel who had not spared me a glance even once, I couldn't tell if he liked me or not" Can we eat now? I'm starving" Gabriel finally spoke, obviously tired of the conversation" Oh yeah sure, go on" Mrs Fidelia said and everyone started eating.

I don't know why but i wanted Gabriel to like me, I didn't want him to hate me, I kept glancing up at him, I watched how he ate his pasta ever so neatly, he picked up his glass of water drinking from it, I watched how he gulped it down and started eating again. He was my cousin and I wasn't supposed to be starring the way I was, yes I know, but I couldn't help it.

I've never seen such a handsome guy before, and the fact I was sitting across him was unreal.

He raised his eyes from his food to meet my eyes. I have been caught starring, I quickly looked down at my food, in the process, I slammed my hand against the plate and the liquid from the food splashed into my eyes. I winced in pain gaining the attention of everyone else

" Are you okay?" Mrs Fidelia asked worriedly before realizing my situation ," Oh my God dear" she panicked " Quickly , Gabriel, take her to go wash her eyes, quickly" she said .   I heard Gabriel grumble some inaudible words before getting up and coming to my side to help me up.

Immediately his hand made contact with my skin, I felt goose-bumps all over my body. He led me to the kitchen and turned on the sink tap, and stepped backwards leaving me to wash my eyes.

I used my hands in washing my eyes but it was a struggle as my hair kept falling into the water, I turned off the water and turned around only to collide into his body.

Chapter 2

I turned off the tap and turned around only to collide into his body, I looked up at his face squinting, still feeling the painful sting in my eyes. He looked at me with folded arms.

"Sorry" I managed to word out "Are you okay now?" He asked and I lowered my head" It still hurts" I said honestly. I heard him sigh before holding me back to the sink, he turned on the tap again and stood behind me, his hands by my sides, his head leaned over my shoulder, while he used his hand in washing my eyes again.

He was so close that his scent became the air I breathe. He used his left hand in brushing the hair from my face over my neck, and over my shoulder to my back, his fingers brushing against my skin in the process, I shivered at the feeling and I felt him pause. I badly wanted to look at his face but decided against it. After a few seconds, he continued, when he was done, he moved away from me, I turned around, some strands of my hair were wet, I looked at him, I could still feel my eyes hurt a little but it was alot better.

"How is it now?" He asked, no readable expression on his face, I just nodded and he immediately turned around to leave, he stopped when he got to the door " Next time, pay more attention to your food" he said without looking at me then he walked out. God, I felt so embarrassed.

Later that night before entering my room, i saw Abel following Gabriel into his room, I knew they were probably going to talk about me, I just hoped they would like me.

I laid on my bed thinking I won't be able to sleep but fortunately, I slept comfortably.

I woke up late the next morning, the time was past 8, I felt I had given a bad impression, I always woke up very early, how come I got so comfortable and woke so late? .

However I quickly brushed my teeth before coming out of my room. The house seemed very quiet, I started climbing down the stairs, that was when I heard Mrs Fidelia's voice, I got down and saw her, she sat on a couch with her phone by her ear as she spoke.

Immediately she saw me, she smiled sweetly, giving me a small wave and I smiled back. She soon hung up the call and stood facing me " How was your night?" She asked, I just nodded " Gabriel and Abel has gone to school, my husband left for work already" she said as she walked to me" I have prepared everything for your school, I don't know if you'll feel comfortable to start tomorrow" she said" You changed my school?" I asked, I really hoped she did.

" Oh yes I did, I figured that school wouldn't be good for you anymore, besides we are very far away from your old home, you'll be going to same school with Gabriel, I hope you are okay with that?" She asked waiting for my reply.

Same school with Gabriel? It was definitely a big school, I was happy. I smiled at her "Yes, I like it" I said and her smile widened" Good then, your food is right there" Mrs Fidelia said pointing to the dinning area." Help yourself, you'll start school tomorrow then, maybe we could go shopping later today, yes?" She asked and I nodded happily.

She patted my shoulder softly before walking back to the couch dialing on her phone again and started talking to someone on the phone again.

I turned to the dinning with a smile as I walked towards it. My life was surely changing for the better, I hope it did. I loved how nice Mrs Fidelia was to me, there was not a single sign of pretence, well not like I was good at detecting when a person lied.

The day was fast, I finished eating and then took my bath, Mrs Fidelia took me out to shop, she bought me alot of girly stuffs, like clothes, shoes, hair pins, scrunchies, make up, jewelries and a lot more, I couldn't be more thankful, she was too nice, she also got me everything I'll need for school, at a point I tried to protest saying it was enough but she wouldn't listen.

We got home to meet Gabriel and Abel already back from school, Abel was doing his school homework, I guessed as he was laid on the floor with books in front of him while he wrote in them.

Gabriel sat operating his phone. I went upstairs to keep every-thing, I heard Mrs Fidelia talking to Gabriel, from the few words I heard, I guessed it was about me going to school with him. I prayed he had no problem with it.

That night however, I couldn't get myself to fall asleep, I was in my pajamas, I laid on my bed starring at the ceiling, I looked at the clock on the small table by my bed, the time was 12:15am. I sighed and stood up. Maybe if I walked around I would be able to find sleep. I don't know how dumb that sounded but well, I was naturally dumb so don't blame me.

I strolled out of my room, the lights in the passage were dim , I got to the stairs and climbed down, I noticed the lights in the kitchen were on, I walked towards it, when I entered I was surprised , Gabriel was there, he was filling a bowl with popcorns, he was on an ash coloured singlet and sweatpants, his hair was a bit rough.

He raised his face to look at me, I blinked "What are you doing awake?" He asked and turned going to keep the rest of the popcorn in the fridge " I couldn't sleep" I muttered.

Chapter 3

" I couldn't sleep" I muttered.He got back to his bowl of popcorn, nodded at me , he picked his bowl and walked past me out of the kitchen, I turned around and walked out of the kitchen as well. Gabriel walked to the living room area, turned on the television, he sat on the floor, not literally , since he had arranged thick blankets on the floor with two pillows, he placed the bowl by his side, he picked up his game remote control in his hand, he was setting the game in the television.

At first I just stood watching, but then I took slow steps until I got into the living area as well, he looked at me, he looked like he was hesitating for a while before tapping the space by his side.   I was glad, he didn't despise me after all, I walked to him and slowly sat down. I starred at the side profile of his face, his muscles flexed as he operated the remote, he looked at me and I immediately looked away, he picked some popcorns with his left hand and put them into his mouth. I was by his left hand side.

" Go ahead and help yourself if you want to" he said referring me to the popcorns.

He was now finally focused on the television screen as he played with full concentration, I started eating the popcorn while watching the game he was playing on the screen and also looking at his face on few occasions.

Then my stupid thought kicked in, I honestly just wanted to help him. I picked a few popcorns in my hand and stretched it towards his mouth. This made him pause.

He looked at me and I froze, I regretted my action, I just wanted to help. "Ummm.... I... I just thought .. you were playing with.. both.. ha... hands, so so.... I thought I... Could .. help by.. by umm feeding you" I stammered innocently.

The expression on his face didn't change, he was frowning, just a little... maybe.. confused and surprised, I couldn't figure it out.

I slowly started retracting my hand, I saw his eyes glance at my hand before looking back at my face." I'm sorry" I said then put the popcorns in my mouth, I lowered my gaze to the floor. I knew he was still starring at me

"Why couldn't you sleep?" I heard him ask and I looked at him again not knowing what to say" Worried about school tomorrow?" He asked. That was probably the reason, I nodded slightly, he sighed.

"Don't be, you'll be fine, they're pretty nice, not everyone though, but I'm sure they'll like you" he assured me then turned back to his game again and resumed playing.

I felt relieved with what he told me. I just sat quietly, I felt him look at me again after a while" You want to play?" He asked and I looked at him." I don't know how to" I said. He sighed" Come, I'll teach you" he spoke calmly stretching his hand towards me." Come"

I didn't know what to do or say, I did like the idea of him teaching me. Maybe he read my mind

" Come closer" he said removing the popcorn from between us and putting it at his right hand side. I shifted closer to him and he held me even closer.

Gabriel put his left hand around my waist as he placed the remote control in my hands and then holding my hands together with the controls. But in a few seconds , maybe he felt the position wasn't good enough to TEACH me.   He went behind me and sat, putting his legs on both my sides, making me sit in between his legs.

His hands went around me holding my hands with the remote control, his head leaned over my shoulder, resting by the side of my face. He soon started instructing me on how to use the remote and how to play the game

But the truth was, I couldn't concentrate, my mind wasn't focused. No boy had ever been this close to me, he was too close. My back was rested against his body, I could smell him and it was nice, his face was just by mine, his hands around my body, wasn't this too much of an intimate position? I mean..... I had accidentally seen a few romantic movies.

I felt goosebumps, I felt hot, my heart thumped aggressively against my rib cage, my body was tense, and I hoped he couldn't hear my heart beat. His whispers by my ear was making me unable to think.

" You get it?" He asked, and I nodded, that was not true, I didn't get anything, he removed his hands from mine telling me to try to play the game, but I just held the remote , I didn't know what to do . I heard him sigh and leaned closer to me this time, taking my hands again" Pay attention" he said softly, his breathing wasn't as relaxed as before, I don't know how I realized that, it was probably just my imagination.

I hoped he wasn't frustrated by me. He started teaching me all-over again, and I tried to pay attention this time but it was really difficult. He told me to try again, I tried this time but I was terrible at it. He took the controls from me and started playing the game by himself as he told me to just watch, he didn't move away, his arms were still around my body.

I watched, I picked from the popcorn, eating them slowly, he played two rounds, I was now feeling sleepy, I allowed my body to fully rest on him, I felt him tense up for a bit, but I was too sleepy to think about it. I just slept off.

Chapter 4

Gabriel's pov

She leaned on me, my heart raced, it had been beating unusually fast since I got into this position with her, I tried to not think about it, I tried to continue playing the game, but my palms were becoming sweaty no matter how many times I wiped it off. I very well knew it was because of her, I looked at her and noticed she had fallen asleep

"Liela?" I called but no reply. Yep, she was asleep, I put down the remote control, her head was now on my chest, slightly bent to the side, her breathing was calm and steady, she was... Beautiful. With that thought, I mentally reminded myself she was my cousin, a relative. Not like I didn't know that before but I felt I should keep it in mind.

I didn't know what to do, I slept here sometimes when I didn't feel like sleeping in my room, but I couldn't let her sleep here with me, especially not on me like this, I didn't want mom to read meanings 'besides this had no meaning' I told myself.

I slowly used my fingers in removing the stray hair that had found it's way to her face, I starred at her face, she was my cousin. I scolded myself.

I slowly lifted her in my arms carrying her bridal style as I stood up , she curled her body further into my arms resting her head on my chest, I starred at her for a while then lifted her up a bit more, I didn't know why I did that, I held her closer making her head fall to the side of my face resting on the crook of my neck, I took a deep breath that came out rough.

I wasn't stupid, I was fully aware of what was going on with me. I walked up the stairs with her in my arms, i took her to her room and tucked her into her bed before turning off the light and walked out of her room.

I went back to the living room to play my game but I was no longer interested in it, I packed up, I picked up the bowl of popcorn remembering how she tried to feed me' She is your cousin, your relative' I told myself.

Liela's pov

I woke up on my bed the next morning, I knew Gabriel was the one who brought me here, thinking of everything that happened last night, I felt slightly embarrassed, today was the day I was to go to school, my new life was about to begin, it had already begun but you know.... School stuff.

I took my bath, got dressed in my uniform, I styled my hair, I took my backpack and stood in front of the mirror ' I think I'm good' I said to myself, I came out of my room, climbed down the stairs, I looked to the dinning and saw everyone already there, eating,   I walked towards them, the first person to see me was Gabriel, his eyes lingered on me for a moment before he looked back to his food and continued eating, he didn't give away any expression.

I couldn't tell if he approved of my look or not, just then Mrs Fi-delia's eyes turned to me" Oh my God Liela...You look so beautiful"

Mrs Fidelia spoke excitedly. And finally, Abel and Mr Noah looked at me.

Abel's mouth opened wide in a "Woah...." He said in disbelieve, it brought a wide smile to my face "You are so beautiful" Abel added. Whew.... Abel didn't hate me" You look good Liela" Mr Noah said and my smile widened even more. I looked at Gabriel if he'll say anything but he didn't, he just kept eating his food.

The smile on my face quickly reduced. I felt I wasn't good enough yet since he didn't compliment me.

"Come, come, come eat, you'll be late for school" Mrs Fidelia said pulling out the chair by her side and I walked to it and sat, hanging my backpack on the chair, I started eating carefully so not to stain my face or my uniform. I stole glances at Gabriel.

Sigh.

Did he not like me? I thought we were okay last night.

Gabriel soon got up from his food, he looked at me, I looked at him realizing we were late "Go dear, you'll be late" Mrs Fidelia said handing me a lunch box, " I packed extra food for you just incase" She said and I took it with a smile. She was too nice. I put the lunch box in my backpack as I stood up.

I wore my backpack, when I looked, I saw that Gabriel had already gotten to the door, opened it and went out. I quickly waved at everyone at the dinning and hurried after him.

There was a black car waiting for us, I don't know what the name of the car was but it looked expensive. Gabriel opened one of the doors of the backseat, threw his bag in and entered, I hurried to the car and entered after Gabriel told me to.

There was a man who looked in his 40's on the drivers seat "Do we move?" The man asked. Gabriel looked at me

" Put on your seatbelt" he instructed, I just starred at him like a dummy, I don't know why I just starred at him like I didn't know what he was talking about. He looked frustrated as he shifted closer to me and stretched to hold the seat belt by my side. My eyes widened at the closeness, he was quick though, he belted me in and pulled away.

My eyes followed him as he sat back in his old position, he sat far away from me, close to the other windscreen " Drive" he ordered and the car started moving just immediately.

We drove out of the compound and into the highway. I looked out of the window looking at the big city.

Chapter 5

My stepmom had been leaving in a secluded area so I was amazed at the beauty of the houses, people, lots of other cars and everything else. I glanced at Gabriel at intervals but he just looked straight ahead. He had wore me the seatbelt but he didn't wear his.

I wanted to start a conversation but I didn't because his face looked too serious, I was scared he'd ignore me or yell at me.

The car finally pulled up in front of a huge building, I guessed it was the school as I saw Gabriel open the door and stepped out. I quickly unbuckled my seat belt and waved at the driver before going out, immediately I got down, the car drove off.

I hurried to Gabriel's side, he stood with his hands in his pockets. I looked up and boldly written above the gate was the school's name * Stay Green int'l school * Wow.... The name made me question but it was really unique, perhaps I'll get used to it and it wouldn't seem so strange anymore.

I saw alot of students going into the school as well, most turned around to look at us ' Was I that attractive?' I thought but then realized it was Gabriel , of cause, I should have known, he was probably the handsome guy in school.

The uniform was a grey coloured skirt/ trouser, white t-shirt and blue jackets, I stood looking at the school. I looked at Gabriel.

He had been waiting, giving me time to take in the environment, he soon started walking into the school, his movement was fast, his left hand holding the strap of his backpack, right hand in his jacket's pocket, I hurried after him trying to keep up, but I'll be honest, I was slightly running

We had gotten into the building and the stares had increased, soon, everyone had gotten into classes. Gabriel stood with me in front of a class "This is your first class for today, take care, I'm sure you'll be fine, I'm getting late for my class" he said and I nodded.

He still wasn't smiling. He starred at me silently for a while and I just dropped my gaze "You look good by the way" he said, I looked at him, an uncontrollable smile forming up on my lips. I saw the side of his lip curl up slightly before he turned around and walked away.With great joy, I stepped into the class.

During lunch break, I came out with the lunch box Mrs Fidelia had given me, when I entered the cafeteria, I saw Gabriel, I wanted to go to him but he sat at a table with about seven other people at the table and there wasn't a spare seat, that was probably his group.

I walked to a different table that was empty and sat down placing the lunchbox on the table, I looked at Gabriel again . He seemed to be having a good time, I could only see his back and a little portion of his face.

They were talking and laughing, I wondered if he was telling them about me and they were laughing at me, I looked away and started eating.

A girl with dark brown curly hair walked to my table " Hi..." She smiled and I smiled back" I'm Marinette" she introduced stretching her hand towards me for a handshake, her smile not fading.

I awkwardly took her hand " Liela" I said softly before taking my hand back. She pulled the chair by my side out and sat with so much energy startling me, I looked at her" Hope you don't mind" Marinette said still smiling and I shook my head then faced my food again and started eating.

"Umm... I saw you come with Gabriel today.." she said. I paused. Of cause, she was here for gossip, I should have known, I looked at her " We're cousins" I said with a bored expression on my face.

She mouthed an Ooh.. while nodding her head, processing what I said. I resumed eating my food. After a very short time, she stood up and walked away. I felt so disappointed, I thought I was going to get a friend. Sigh.

I looked at Gabriel and saw he was looking at me, after few seconds he turned back to his friends. I thought he was going to come over or ask me to join them , but that never happened.

When it was time to go home, the driver came again, I wore my seat belt by myself this time, and just like before, we didn't speak any word to each other throughout the drive home.

Chapter 6

We got home that day and I went to my room, not too long, I heard a knock on my door, I got up and walked to the door, I opened it and Gabriel was standing right in front of me with an expressionless face.

"Hi" I said not knowing what else to say" Mom sent for you" he said and walked away.

I hurried after him, we both climbed down the stairs, Mrs Fidelia was standing in the living room all dressed up like she was going for a business trip, a luggage box was by her side. Abel sat on one of the sofa.

When we got to the living room, Mrs Fidelia stretched a box towards me, I looked at it, a phone was drawn on the carton. "Here Liela, I got you a phone" she told me smiling, I reached for it and took it, I was happy, confused, surprised, I didn't know what to say

" I knew you didn't have one, so I decided to get you one" she smiled. I smiled back" Thank you so much ma" I said as I bowed my head slightly then raised it up again " thank you" I repeated.

She waved her hand " Don't thank me please, it's fine" she spoke kindly." My number is in it already, my husband's, Abel's and.... Gabriel's number too" She told me, I wasn't sure if I just imagined it or not, but I felt she stressed on Gabriel's name in particular.

I looked at Gabriel who had gone to sit on the couch and was operating his phone, I looked back at Mrs Fidelia "If you ever need anything at anytime, or anything happens, you can always call any of us, okay?" She said and I nodded with a smile.

"I'm going on a business trip, your uncle wouldn't be back for some time, I'm sorry I didn't tell you all on time but I'll be out for a week, so... I'll employ a cook to..." I didn't let her finish" I can cook" I said, I didn't look at Abel and Gabriel but I felt their eyes turn to me" You can cook?" Mrs Fidelia asked like she didn't understand.

I nodded anyway" I've been cooking since I was 9, and I think I'm pretty good at it, I can handle the cooking" I said" You don't have to bother yourself Liela" Mrs Fidelia tried to brush me off" I would really like to handle the cooking till you return, I don't find cooking stressful at all" I tried to sound as convincing as possible.

She sighed then gave a small nod." Okay" she approved " But if you ever feel like it's too much to handle, give me a call and I'll send you guys a cook okay?"

I nodded even though I knew I wouldn't call her

"I already prepared dinner, it's in the fridge, so y'all can eat when you want to, okay?" She said"Okay"   Mrs Fidelia walked to Abel and held him up to his feet, she hugged him and gave him a kiss on the forehead, she moved to Gabriel opening her arms. He looked at her" Mom....." He complained.

Mrs Fidelia frowned and started pulling him up. He reluctantly stood up and she hugged him, he hugged her back." Don't be like that Gabriel, I don't care how much you've grown, I'm your mother and you're my son, understand?" She said while withdrawing from him and Gabriel nodded with a forced smile.

Mrs Fidelia held her hands up silently asking him to lower his head, he bent his back slightly bringing himself lower and Mrs Fidelia held his face placing a kiss on his forehead. I smiled, the sight was funny and cute

" Be a good boy" she told him before walking over to me, giving me a hug and a kiss on the forehead, making my smile widen." If you need any help with your phone, you can ask Gabriel" she said and I nodded glancing at Gabriel, he also looked at me " I'll be leaving now" she turned to her sons " Boys, you better take care of Liela okay? She's a girl, don't make her feel lonely either,treat her like an egg, alright?" Mrs Fidelia lectured.

" Okay..." Abel said loudly. While Gabriel just nodded slightly. She waved us all goodbye before she left. Mrs Fidelia was the nicest person I had ever met in my life, I looked at the phone in my hands, I was 16 years old, will be 17 soon, I've never had a phone before. I was very happy

" Egg" I heard Abel say, distracting me from my thoughts, I looked at him, " Egg, you should go rest" Abel said and my eyes widened. Was he calling me an egg? I didn't know what to do." Don't.. don't call me that.. again" I said and I heard the most beautiful laugh ever, Gabriel chuckled, I looked at him shocked, he just sat there with one side of his lips pulled up, that was the first time I saw him smile, he looked extremely handsome, " I have to call you that, so I'll remember to treat you like an egg" Abel replied.

I looked at him not knowing what to say, I looked at Gabriel again and he was still looking at me with that half smile" I.. I... I'll go... Up.. upstairs" I stammered and immediately turned around climbing up the stairs in haste.

" Have a good rest, egg" Abel shouted and again I heard Gabriel's laugh but the sound was faint, I hurried to my room.

Why was I feeling so nervous or no, embarrassed, or was that me being shy under Gabriel's stare? . I walked to my bed allowing my self fall on it, I glanced at the phone again. I had Gabriel's number, I couldn't help but wonder if he had mine too.

Chapter 7

Immediately the time was 6:00pm, I went down, took the food from the fridge, heated it up and dished it out, I set the dinning. Before I could go call Gabriel and Abel, I saw them both coming downstairs and I just waited.

They got down and Abel hurried to me, the time now was almost 7pm, " Egg, you prepared dinner already?" He asked looking at the dinning table, I nodded at him with a small smile, ignoring the fact that he still called me egg, Abel hurried to the dinning and soon started eating.

Gabriel walked up to me, he looked like he was about to say something but he didn't, he walked past me and took his seat at the table and began to eat, I stood watching them" Are you not eating?" Abel asked, and Gabriel looked at me, I walked to them, took my seat and ate..When we were done eating, I took the plates to go wash. Abel offered to help me, probably wanting to treat me like the egg he calls me, I told him not to worry and washed them myself.

I went to Abel's room to make sure he was asleep but well...he wasn't, I told him I wanted to treat him like an elder sister does but he laughed saying he's never had an elder sister. I decided to show him.

I told him a kids bed time story, he thinks it's funny saying he's not a child. I then decided to formulate an action story with alot of fights in it. He seemed to like it, I gave him a forehead kiss and turned off his room light before walking out and closing the door behind me.

Abel liked me alot and I really appreciated it. I turned around and Gabriel was standing in front of his room door which was just opposite Abel's. I blinked. His back was rested against the door." You shouldn't stress yourself out" Gabriel spoke calmly. ' Did he care about me or just doesn't want me to get along with Abel?' " I'm not" i said" Go to bed now then, we have school tomorrow, go rest" he spoke again calmly" I only prepared dinner and put Abel to bed, I'm not tired, you should go to bed too" I said trying to be stubborn

Gabriel tilted his head to the side slowly, his eyes fixed on me making me a bit nervous" So what now? You want to put me to bed too?" He asked looking serious.   I blinked, suddenly feeling uncomfortable. He slowly straightened his head again waiting for my response but I didn't know what to say" Go to bed, you took care of Abel, I should take care of you" Gabriel spoke sounding a little annoyed.

And just like every other time, my stupidity kicked in" What now? You want to put me to bed?" I asked stepping forward and folding my arms across my chest. The side of Gabriel's lip pulled up forming a mischievous smile "You want me to?" He asked removing his body from the door.

I unfolded my arms " Forget it" "Good night" I added before hurrying to my room. I walked to my bed and laid down pulling the blanket over my body all the way to my neck

'Why do I keep feeling nervous around him?' I thought to myself, I keep feeling shy, embarrassed and mostly nervous. When he's nice to me, I feel very happy, when he doesn't talk to me, I feel sad, if he's close... I feel goosebumps, I feel hot. The whole thing was weird to me, I've only been here for three days.

I woke up early to prepare breakfast, it got ready before the boys woke up, they were already dressed in their uniforms when they came down, I was also already dressed.

We all sat at the dinning eating, it was quiet all through except Abel who kept praising my cooking skills. Ummm okay that's to say it wasn't totally quiet. Gabriel did not say anything. When we were done, I took the plates back to the kitchen, Abel's driver took him to school while I and Gabriel also went to school as usual.

One week had soon gone by, Gabriel and I talked sometimes, he never smiled at me, but I was getting along with Abel very well, I still had no friend in school, I was okay with it tho, I was already used to it, at least no one tried to bully me either. It was just one more week before Mrs Fidelia and Mr Noah comes back home.

It was a Monday, myself and Gabriel got to school like every other day, I hurried after him immediately we came down from the car. He was walking too fast. He suddenly Stopped walking, I didn't realize it on time, so I ended up colliding into his back. I hear him sigh.

I stepped backwards and raised my face to look at him as he turned to face me, he was frowning" Do you ever focus?' he asked still frowning down at me, I looked around and some students were looking, some murmuring, I heard some ask themselves if we were fighting, I looked back at Gabriel and frowned "You were walking too fast" I complained not caring if I sounded childish.

His frown faded for only a second but returned quickly" Why are you following me, can't you be by yourself? You don't need to stick around with me. Just act like you don't know me when we're in school from now on" he said and started walking away leaving me.

I felt so sad, I saw some students around especially the girls, they laughed amongst themselves looking at me. I ignored and just walked into school slowly, I couldn't figure out why he suddenly said that, was he embarrassed by me? Well, I'll just be alone then.

Chapter 8

The time went by very slowly, I and Gabriel both had maths class together, I sat in front of the class, he sat behind. I tried my best not to look at him through out the entire class, once the bell for lunch break was rang, I slowly packed my books into my bag.

I left the class just like everyone else, I walked into the Hall way, there were only a few people. I suddenly felt a sharp pain in my lower belly and I bent down holding the wall for support . The pain was slowly fading off when I heard a male voice." Are you okay?" The voice asked.Slowly I raised my head to look, it was a boy, handsome, black hair, thin lips, brown eyes" Are you alright?" He asked again and I nodded.

Before I knew it, he was helping me up as the pain had subsided." Thanks" I said, his hands still on my shoulder" Do you need to go to the clinic?" He asked and I shook my head." No". He nodded at that

" I'm Harry" he introduced" Liela" I said with a smile and he nodded returning the smile" You sure you're okay?" He asked and again I nodded" What grade are you in?" Harry asked" 12th grade" I replied" Me too, you're new here I'm guessing" he spoke with a smile and yes, I nodded again" Have any friends yet? I could be a friend" he offered still smiling and I quickly nodded happily" No friends, just my cousin who umm" I paused thinking it wasn't necessary" Your cousin?" Harry asked wanting me to continue.

I sighed "Yeah... He just doesn't want me around" I said sadly. I saw Harry nod, he seemed like he was thinking about something for a while "Gabriel?" He asked all of a sudden and I nodded quickly surprised at how he knew who my cousin was "Ah.. I guessed right, I overheard people talking about Gabriel's cousin who's now in the school, a girl, just didn't know it was you, I also never thought she was this beautiful" Harry said with a charming smile.

I smiled, I felt flattered "Thank you" I said dropping my gaze a bit shy. "Welcome gorgeous, so... We're friends?" He asked stretching his hand for a handshake and I took it, he later released my hand, giving me a small nod before walking away.

Yay..... I had a friend, boy or not, he was my friend.

When school was over for the day. I and Gabriel were in the car going home, as usual we were both quiet, I didn't like it, we couldn't be like this forever" I made a friend today" I spoke breaking the silence , a smile on my face as I looked at Gabriel, he looked at me " Good for you" Gabriel replied and looked forward again. " You were right, people are nice, I was passing through a bad pain and he came to me" I said, taking note of how Gabriel looked at me immediately

"What happened to you?" He asked worriedly and my smile widened, he did care about me" Just a stomach pain, but it stopped immediately" I said, he just nodded." So... This very handsome guy came to me... He said his name was Harry" I spoke excitedly. Gabriel didn't say anything, he just maintained the frown on his face as he looked away from me" He was very nice" I added and kept narrating everything that happened between me and Harry, Gabriel didn't even comment on it once, and it made me sad. When I had nothing else to say, I stopped talking and again we fell into silence.

We got home as usual, I prepared lunch and we all ate, Abel once again praised my cooking, we also ate dinner later that day and went to our rooms, Gabriel ignored me completely. I was too sad, I didn't know if I should talk to him about it or not.

Two days past, although I and Harry were now friends, we didn't hang out much, a girl named Theresa came up to me during one of our classes and asked to be my friend. I came home from school with Gabriel and found out I was having my period, it was already evening and I had to prepare dinner. I was having very bad cramps but I had already promised Mrs Fidelia that I would handle the cooking, I didn't want to back out.

I was on my pajamas which were a bit baggy, I came out of my room and walked down the hall holding unto my lower belly in pain, I walked slightly bent, when I got to the stairs, I looked down to the living room and saw Abel watching a show in the television while Gabriel was operating his phone. I didn't want them to know something was wrong with me, so I tried my best to stand up straight, I started taking very slow steps down the stairs, by the time I got to the ground, they still hadn't noticed me, so I just walked straight into the kitchen.

Once I got in, I bent holding my belly again. God, it was terrible, I opened the pantry and picked out a pan but too bad, I wasn't careful enough, it slipped out of my hand and fell to the ground, bouncing a few times, the sound ringing loudly. I bit my lip hoping they didn't hear it.

But not even that kind of miracle was impossible. Both Gabriel and Abel hurried into the kitchen to find me holding the counter top for support as I tried to pick the pan from the floor.

Chapter 9

"Are you okay?" I heard Gabriel ask as he walked up to me, stopping me from picking the pan, he held me to face him, his eyes running all over my body, probably checking for..... Injuries? Well he should be checking the pan." Are you okay?" He asked again and I nodded. Abel picked up the pan and placed it on the counter top then walked to my side waiting for my answer" I'm fine" I said still unable to stand straight holding my stomach.

Gabriel was silent starring at me, I raised my head to look at his face" You want to see a doctor?" He asked. I shook my head " No, it's just a stomach pain" I replied" A stomach pain? You still have to see a doctor" Gabriel insisted and Abel nodded in agreement.I sighed" I'm fine, it's not really a stomach pain, it's just..." I trailed off " I'll be okay" I added.

Gabriel exhaled and without warning, he lifted me from the ground and put me on the counter to sit. I starred at him with wide eyes. "What.. what are you doing?" I asked a bit flustered" You'll sit here and tell us what to do. Okay?" He instructed" But.. look.. no, I.." I tried to object but he interrupted "Just listen Liela, you tell us what to do, okay?" Gabriel insisted and I just nodded.

Not long, they were turning on the gas cookers, putting the pan on it, cracking eggs, bringing out seasonings, slicing vegetables etc. All with my instructions, I swear I couldn't be more thankful to them.

I watched as Gabriel was doing most of the cooking while Abel assisted by bringing out stuff and lending Gabriel items and also checking on me, Abel was too sweet.

Gabriel pulled up his sleeves, sometimes swinged his head trying to get his hair off his face, I couldn't help but smile. At a point Gabriel walked to me and stood in front of me, his hair had fallen into his face again, he put his hands backward as they were wet, he brought his face forward close to me.

At first I blinked, although I knew what he was asking me to do, but God, he was too good looking, I just starred at him before I slowly lifted my hands to his face slowly using my fingers to brush the hair out of his face and put them behind his ears, not all were long enough but at least, they could stay out of his face. All this while he starred into my eyes and I did same, even when I was done I still left my hand on his face untill..

"What are you two doing?" Abel asked, his voice making us look at him almost immediately. I looked to the ground awkwardly while Gabriel cleared his throat as he walked away from me and back to what he was doing. Gabriel looked at Abel who was still giving him a questioning look "What's it Abel? I asked her for help with my hair, get back to work" Gabriel said irritated and finally Abel looked away.

They finished cooking. The food was a little bit too spicy but we all laughed over it and ate it anyway. I put Abel to bed and since I didn't see Gabriel go to his room, I came back to the living room to check and yep, I was right, he was in the living room, I walked to him.

He was playing his video game with everything arranged on the floor except for the popcorns." Should I get you snacks?" I asked, he looked at me " No" he replied and faced his game again." How do you feel now?" He asked still playing his game" Better" I replied taking the opportunity to sit by him, I sat very close to him. He stopped and looked at me. I shifted from him just a bit thinking he didn't want me near him but he didn't stop staring at me

" I want to call Mom since I don't know what to do to... Ahm... Help you with... I mean..." Gabriel said finding it hard to speak " Nevermind" he stopped and looked back at his game but didn't continue playing.   It only just registered to me that he might know what was wrong with me." I'm okay now" I muttered feeling embarrassed" Um thank you for.... Helping me out today" I added.

Gabriel didn't reply me for about two minutes, but then he suddenly put down his remote control and turned to me completely " Do you think I treat you badly?" He asked.' What kind of question was that?' I thought. Actually he did treat me badly sometimes, but whenever he does something nice, it just seems to cover up for all the bad he's done before and I just can't feel sad, I didn't know how to answer I just lowered my gaze.

" I'm sorry for the times I've been unreasonable, I'll be better" he said and I looked at him" No, it's fine, you've been nice to me, it's just me who's... Who's been stupid" I said bowing my head again unable to look at him. I knew he was starring at me even without looking at him

" Be careful with Harry" was the next thing I heard, I quickly raised my gaze to meet Gabriel's " You know him?" I asked " Yes, why not? I've been in the school for a long time, well he's not a very good person, I'm not saying you... should..." He said facing his game again.

I wanted him to continue, I was happy he was caring about me and actually talking to me, I didn't think before doing what I did, I shifted closer and held his face with both my hands to look at me. I paused realizing what I did, my hands still on his face

"Umm.. I, I'm sorry" I said slowly removing my hands. Gabriel smiled at me, I didn't expect that, he held both my hands removing them from his face but held them in his hands "You're very active aren't you?" He asked with a smile.

Chapter 10

I felt so embarrassed and dropped my gaze. " I'm sorry, I didn't think before I...." I was saying but he interrupted me " it's fine" he assured with a little laugh afterwards

" I just wanted you to continue what you were saying" I managed to say. He didn't say anything but kept caressing my hands that were still in his. I lifted my eyes to see his face , he was staring at me. We both remained quiet for a while.

" You should go to bed Liela" Gabriel said breaking the silence. I've been looking for a way to leave anyway, I quickly got up nodding, I hurried towards the stairs but then turned to him, he had also turned to look at me" Can I talk to you in school?" I asked hopefully, I saw his smile widen and he nodded once with a blink.

A smile quickly spread on my lips even tho I tried to hold it back, I turned around and ran up the stairs happily. God how come Gabriel could control my moods this easily.

The next day came quickly, it was two more days left before Mrs Fidelia and Mr Noah would return.

I sat alone in the cafeteria, not long before Theresa came to join me, I was glad I now had a friend. I had also found out that Theresa and Harry were siblings, Which made me wonder if it was Harry who told Theresa to be my friend, it made me a little sad that we wouldn't have been friends if not for Harry, but I wasn't sure tho.

A lot of students were in the cafeteria eating and talking, Gabriel was not here yet and I just couldn't help looking around

"Looking for Harry?" Theresa asked, I looked at her and shook my head rapidly "Who?" She asked with a smile " Gabriel" I murmured and she nodded" He might have gone out with girls, you know, he's very popular among the girls" Theresa said. I looked at her, not understanding what she was driving at" I guess" I whispered to my self immediately I understood what she was saying, I suddenly felt sad, God, I didn't even know why I was sad.

" My brother isn't like that tho" Theresa spoke again. I looked at her again. What was she insinuating? I was a bit annoyed but I just ignored and started eating my food.

Soon Gabriel walked into the cafeteria, his right hand in his pocket, I raised my head and my eyes met his, I immediately felt glued to the spot starring into his blue eyes. From the corner of my eye I saw Theresa arranging her hair and dress, it bothered me a little but I kept my gaze on Gabriel, he started walking again heading towards.... Me

" Hey Liela" I heard from behind me and I looked away from Gabriel, right by my side was Harry, he had a smile plastered on his face, I looked up at him, then looked back at Gabriel, Gabriel had stopped coming towards me and wasn't even looking at me anymore, he walked to a different table, to the table where his supposed friends were, he shook hands with a few of them as they spoke before he sat down, his back now facing me.

I felt a sting of pain hit me, I thought he was coming to meet me, or was it..... I looked at Harry

"Are you alright?" Harry asked, his smile slowly fading, I quickly nodded." Yes, I'm fine" I lied" May I sit?" He asked and again I nodded. He sat, I didn't know why but I wasn't comfortable sitting with two siblings as my friends, it felt weird, but honestly that wasn't all that bothered me.

We got home that day. Abel was already home, Gabriel just went straight upstairs while I talked to Abel, Abel asked me what was wrong with Gabriel , but even I had no idea. Gabriel came down to eat lunch with us but when it was time for dinner, he didn't come down, I and Abel went to his room to call him but he didn't open the door, he told us to leave and that he wasn't hungry.

It was another morning again. I was dressed for school, Abel was ready too, we both sat and ate alone, again Gabriel didn't come down to eat, both I and Abel had become worried, I told Abel to go to school promising to check up on Gabriel before Abel agreed to leave.

Once Abel had gone for school, I took the plates to the kitchen before climbing upstairs, I got to Gabriel's room and stood in front of the door. I was scared, I knocked on the door, but there was no reply, I knocked again and...

"The door is opened" was what I heard Gabriel say. I took a deep breath before slowly opening the door and stepping in. The room was a little dark, only a dull blue light was on making everything in the room blue, he hadn't opened his window curtains yet. He was still laid under his blanket.

"Gabriel?" I called as I walked to the side of his bed "What?" He asked, his voice sounding grumpy" We're getting late for school, you didn't eat last night and also didn't come down to eat this morning, are you okay?" I asked" I won't be going to school today" He said ignoring the other things I said.

I stood wondering why he wasn't going to school "Why?" I asked.

Gabriel pushed the blanket from his face and looked at me " I'm not well" he said. I immediately felt worried " I'll stay home too" I said" No, go to school" Gabriel countered raising his upper body from the bed using his elbows as support " I can't go if you're not going" I said bowing my head slightly " Why?" He asked softly

" I...I.., I don't want anyone to question me of your where about" I lied, I just didn't want to stay away from him, and as stupid as that sounds, it remains the truth.

Gabriel sat up, I could now see the white singlet he had on and the outlines of his muscles. Jeez what was wrong with me?

Chapter 11

I stared at him, his hair was a mess, of cause he was just waking up, but he looked even more handsome "Are you sure? You don't have to worry tho, no one would ask you about me, I've already informed my friends I wouldn't be in school, they'd help inform the school, they'd only ask about me from my friends not you, so go to school, you're late already, go" Gabriel said, I didn't want to go, he was sick, I had to take care of him.

"Umm I'm still staying" I Insisted and Gabriel gave me a questioning look " Why? He asked again " I... I. Can't .... leave you home alone when you're sick" I stammered, Gabriel immediately threw his leg down from the bed. I wasn't expecting the sudden movement so I flinched moving backward, I thought he was going to hit me just like my step mother did.

Gabriel sat there watching me before reaching his hand for me, he held my wrist and pulled me towards himself, since I was still a bit unstable I moved towards him with a stager and fell on him, I don't know when or how but I found myself leaning on Gabriel, my hands resting on the upper part of his chest and his hands holding my waist, I looked down at him and he starred back at me.....

Gabriel's Pov

She told me she couldn't leave me alone at home since I was sick, but looking at her I could tell that wasn't all, there was definitely more to why she didn't want to go to school, I put my legs down from the bed, since I wasn't actually sick I wanted to convince her to leave me alone at home, but she flinched moving away from me.

I stopped to look at her, did she think I'd hit her? She looked..... Scared?. I regretted stepping down like that, I remained sitting on the bed, I wanted her to know I'd never hurt her

I reached for her, I wanted to apologise, I held unto her wrist and pulled her to myself, I didn't intend to use so much force but well.... It just happened, I just didn't want her so far away.

To my own shock, Liela moved too easily, like she had no bone in her, she stumbled to me and not being able to balance herself, she ended up falling on me.

My hands quickly flew to hold her from falling but I ended up holding her waist, her hands pressed against my upper chest for support, her knees rested on the edge of the bed in the little space in between my legs, I looked up at her still in my sitting position, her head a bit higher than mine, some strands of her hair had fallen to the side, softly tickling the side of my face and neck.

I starred directly into her beautiful brown eyes, I felt enchanted, she starred back at me, blinking once in a while, her cheeks flushed pink. We remained there.' God, she is beautiful' I thought , I didn't know how long we've been like this, all I could think about was her, the fact she was between my legs was not helping matters, she was dressed in her uniform, while I was just on a singlet and sweatpants, her fingers touching my bare skin.

Her tensed body had started relaxing, our faces were only inches apart, my hands itched to move around her body, my lips itching to meet hers' What in the world was going on with me?' I asked myself, I started reciting that she was my cousin in my head but it wasn't doing anything to stop what I felt.

How did I start feeling this way towards her, the knowledge that she was my relative was supposed to automatically be in my head, therefore nothing would make me attracted to her, that's how the bond between siblings worked, but NO, it wasn't working right now, I was very much attracted to Liela which I knew was very wrong, God! I couldn't help myself, she had to pull away, if she stayed any longer I don't know what I'd do, I don't know how long I could control myself.

I was already getting a fucking erection, and she didn't seem to be making any attempt to pull away. I might decide to kiss her now, it was taking all my will power not to move, I licked my bottom lip " Liela..." I muttered, my voice hoarse, God! I sounded terrible.

She blinked , then cleared her throat, she moved, My hands suddenly tightened on her waist, although I knew she had to get up, my body wanted the opposite

"Gabriel. I..... I.... Should stand up" she said almost whispering, I nodded but my hands still did not loosen from her waist. I finally let go when she started getting up, her knees brushed against my dick while she was trying to stand up, and I let out a hiss, I hardened the more, immediately she was up I got up too turning my back at her , I couldn't let her see my erection.

"You should go change from your uniform since you won't be going to school" I said trying to dismiss her." Oh. Yea..yeah, your food is on the dinning, I'll be back" She said awkwardly before hurrying away.

I let out the breadth I've been holding and let my self sit back on the bed. I had to stop these feelings somehow, I can't keep getting turned on every moment I'm alone with her, it hadn't even been up to a month since she got here, although I was 18, she was just 16, her 17th birthday was not that far away tho

" Gabriel she's your fucking cousin" I told myself but stopped knowing it was useless. Letting out a sigh, I had to go out, I didn't want her to come back here.

I came out of my room and headed down the stairs towards the dinning. Once I got there, I pulled out the chair and sat, my mind drifted to her again but I shook my head trying to get her out of my mind.

Chapter 12

Gabriel's Pov

I sat at the dinning holding the spoon and looking at the food in front of me, I didn't feel like eating. I raised my head and saw Liela walking towards me. She had changed from her uniform, she was now on black leggings and a camisole, her straight hair let down with small curls at the tip. Her curves swayed slightly as she walked, my lips parted in admiration. I looked away feigning nonchalance. I didn't get it, my entire body responded to her presence

'Bad' I thought, I knew being with her alone in the house especially her being close wouldn't be easy for me. She walked to me and pulled out the chair in front of mine and sat "You like it?" She asked with a smile. I gulped and looked away, that smile was doing things to me, awakening my nerves.

"I don't really have the appetite" I said truthfully. She nodded

"That's because you're sick" she said. Nope, I wasn't sick.

She stood up walking around the table towards me . My whole body became alert, anticipating her closeness. She got to me and stood behind me.

" I should give you a massage, maybe it would help" she said softly and I sat up straighter, all the hairs on my body standing up, I could feel her closeness.

Immediately Liela's hands touched my shoulders and squeezed a little, I felt current run through every vein in my body, and going down to the member between my legs, making me harden all over

I immediately stood up and turned to her, holding her hands away from me, I felt breathless. She looked at me, confusion written all over her face and a little bit of sadness. ' God she obviously had no idea what she was doing to me' I starred at her. If she touched me again, I'd loose it for sure.

Liela stepped forward and I stepped back, holding her hands and pushing her backwards softly, I licked my lip, I didn't know what to tell her, I was acting weird to her and I knew that

" Liela" I said, my voice sounding the deepest and most breath-less I've ever sounded. God, I cursed within myself when I heard how I sounded, Liela was sure doing things to my body. I needed to get away from her, I had no idea why my body was reacting extra today, I mean I've been getting these feelings whenever I was with her but today felt extra, I was almost not able to handle myself.

It was probably because we were only and my senses knew no one else was in the entire house but just us." Liela, don't come close to me" I warned finally letting go of her hand. " Did I do something wrong?" Liela asked, she looked like she was going to cry." No no no, I promise you're really great, you didn't do anything, it's completely me, I need...." I paused and cleared my throat, my voice still very deep and hoarse

"I want to rest, I'll be upstairs, I need to rest" I said" Are you sure?" She asked moving towards me again. I moved back holding my hand in front of me as a sign for her to stop coming close and she did stop"You are not okay, you should take drugs" Liela suggested worriedly"Look, I've caught a cold, I don't want you to contact it" I lied and applauded myself in my head, that sounded like a good excuse

"Please leave me alone and don't call Mom or anyone, I'll be fine, okay?" I said. She didn't reply, just starred at me. I made her feel bad but I really had to do this, I took the opportunity to leave, I turned around and walked away, I climbed up the stairs and entered my room. I locked the door and let myself fall on the bed.

Although she was my cousin, my body didn't seem to understand that. I needed to make it clear to every inch of me, every organ in me had to understand that Liela is my cousin and we shouldn't be feeling things cause we wouldn't be doing anything with her.   I wanted to be with her, I couldn't stop thinking about her honestly, every single time I tried staying away, I just couldn't

Just then it occurred to me it wasn't just my body who needed to understand this, my mind knew this but I still couldn't stop the thoughts of her. Was it my.... Heart? God No. I realized how I felt about her, I couldn't stop thinking about how happy she was when she talked about Harry, it didn't sit well with me at all, was I jealous?

No no no no no, this wasn't good. My heart needed to stop, it wasn't just my body . My whole being was just simply refusing to accept that Liela was my cousin. I needed to distract myself and I knew exactly what to do.

Chapter 13

I decided not to disturb Gabriel throughout, I just watched movies to pass time, Later Abel came back from school, I prepared lunch and Gabriel finally came down to eat, and also for dinner.

The next day was a Saturday, it was already noon, I sat in my room operating my phone but got bored , I decided to go down stairs , on getting down. Abel and Gabriel were playing video games, they were competing against each other, and from the looks of things, Abel was failing miserably.

I always do things without thinking so don't be surprised, I walked to the front of the screen blocking them from seeing the game, Abel grumbled loudly while Gabriel just stopped playing, looking at me with one eyebrow raised.

Okay, I don't know why I did this, I kept quiet feeling awkward and stupid

" Get away from there Liela, can't you see we're on serious business?"

Abel complained, he was obviously annoyed. I however stood my ground" I'm not letting you both play this game" I said. Gabriel leaned back on the couch resting his back and dropping his remote control before folding his arms against his chest tilting his head slightly to the side.

I gulped nervously, his intense stare making me think twice on my action " Gabriel are you not saying anything?" Abel turned to Gabriel in frustration seeking for help. At first Gabriel did not reply but afterwards he spoke.

" Liela" he started. The way he called my name made adrenaline run down my spine, this was getting even more awkward.

We weren't all that close yet, so why did I even make this foolish attempt?.

" What do you think you're doing?" Gabriel asked" I um I don't want to be alone in my room" I said half truthfully and dropped my gaze in embarrassment.

" Oh... Mom did say we should treat her like an egg" Abel said now smiling, I quickly looked at him" Abel don't start" I warned but he only laughed

Gabriel got up and walked to me" Hey" he spoke now standing right in front of me, I craned my neck to look at him. He slowly cupped my face in his hands looking down at me " You're a little too active Liela" he teased, his voice soft, I blinked just then we were both separated by Abel. He pushed Gabriel away from me and stood between us.

" Stop getting so close to her Gabriel" Abel said making me a little more embarrassed" What.. what... What are.. you talking about?" I stuttered.

Abel sighed " I'm here too, shouldn't I get some attention too?" Abel asked and I couldn't help but laugh, I looked at Gabriel, he had just a small smile on.

I was about to speak when the door opened, we all looked,it was Mrs Fidelia and Mr Noah who entered with their luggages, we must have been very distracted as we didn't hear them enter the compound.

They paused to look at us "What's going on?" Mrs Fidelia asked with a smile. Only then did we realize our position,

" It's all good, welcome back home" Gabriel said as he moved to them then Abel followed, I just stood there not knowing what to do. They settled in and Mrs Fidelia wanted to cook so I decided to assist her .

We were both in the kitchen, I was slicing carrots while Mrs Fidelia was stirring something in the pot " Liela, how did you cope, hope my son's didn't give you any trouble?" Mrs Fidelia asked not looking at me. I glanced at her " No ma, they were very nice to me, they helped me alot" I said" Oh really? Tell me about it" Mrs Fidelia spoke now looking at me, I looked at her

" They... Did help me cook on a particular day when I wasn't feeling too well" I said " Really? You fell sick?" She asked, worry in her tune " No, it... It. It was just my period" I said feeling embarrassed, I turned back to the carrots and continued slicing" Oh I see" Mrs Fidelia muttered and turned back to stirring what's in the pot " How come they've never helped me even when I ask for their help, they must really care about you" She added

A small smile appeared on my face on hearing that. We were both quiet for a while until..." How is your relationship with Gabriel?" Mrs Fidelia asked breaking the silence. I didn't expect her to ask that, I got nervous and accidentally cut my finger slightly , I winced in pain dropping the knife immediately .

Mrs Fidelia hurried to my side and took my hand in hers " Are you okay?" She asked worriedly, I nodded, the finger now bleeding. I put the bleeding finger in my mouth sucking on it

" Come with me" Mrs Fidelia said as she led me out of the kitchen " Gabriel...." Mrs Fidelia called with urgency in her voice. I saw Gabriel's head pop out from above a couch in the living room, he was probably lying down, he quickly got up and walked to us " It's just a small cut ma, I'll be fine" I said to Mrs Fidelia now removing my finger from my mouth but she ignored

" What happened to her?" Gabriel asked sounding a little worried, " She cut herself" Mrs Fidelia reported to Gabriel " please help me treat the cut for her so I can continue in the kitchen" She added. " I'm okay, I can still continue cooking, it's only a small cut" I tried to explain

" A small cut that's bleeding" Gabriel said holding my hand up showing it to me " I'll take her from here mom" Gabriel said to Mrs Fidelia and held my arm, he led me to the living room while Mrs Fidelia went back into the kitchen.

Gabriel made me sit on a couch " I'm fine Gabriel, really" I said trying to convince him to forget the treatment. " Just keep quiet" he said calmly, he walked away from me to a shelf and brought out a first aid box, then walked back to me.

He sat by me on the couch making me face him. He set the box on the stool close to the couch, only now did my eyes decide to examine him.

He had on combat trousers and a tight singlet, his abs well defined in the singlet, his hair messy like he's ran his hands through it a couple times, he looked as handsome as always if not more.

After Gabriel set down the things he probably needed, he turned back to me and took my hand, my left hand, my index finger was the one with the cut" Is it going to hurt?" I asked, scared, "Are you scared?" Gabriel asked, his eyes on my injured finger, he raised his eyes to look at my face when I didn't answer immediately.

My eyes were already teary, I slowly nodded once with a little " uhm" sound. He sighed and shifted closer to me still holding my hand in his." It wouldn't hurt much" he said but it didn't reduce the fear in me. I just remained silent looking at him, his eyes remained on me too.

He slowly lifted my hand and soon put my injured finger in his mouth slowly sucking on it, as he kept eye contact with me

My eyes widened, I didn't know if this was part of the treatment, this wasn't supposed to be part of the treatment right? I felt tingles rush down my body from my finger. My cheeks flushed bright pink, I had sucked on that same finger few minutes ago and now he was doing same, I couldn't remember if he saw me. I blinked and tried pulling my hand away but he didn't let me

" Relax" he said, my finger still in his mouth, his eyes on my face, I gulped, I blinked, I shifted on my seat uncomfortably. He finally removed my finger from his mouth, his eyes not leaving my face, he used his thumb in brushing softly across the cut spot of my finger and I shivered in response. I couldn't hold his stare anymore.

I bowed my face looking at other places trying to avoid Gabriel's eyes, but he was making it hard for me.

His gaze boring holes in my face "Done" I heard him say. I looked at him again surprised, then lifted my finger to look at my hand.

Chapter 14

I was shocked at what I saw, the whole of my index finger was bandaged. I starred at it not knowing what to say, I glanced at Gabriel then my finger again" But... But... But, it was just a small cut, why my whole finger?" I asked confused, I saw his lip pull up in a smile.

"Aren't you grateful I didn't bandage you entire hand?" Gabriel asked still starring at my face, I opened my mouth to speak but nothing came out, " But" I tried again but Gabriel got up, he was obviously laughing at me, he turned to go, I stood up quickly and held his arm looking up at him.

" Gabriel please.., this is so embarrassing" I said showing him how big my finger looked because of the bandage." Liela, leave it that way" Gabriel said, his smile widening. I knew he was doing this on purpose.

"Please...."I begged "No" he replied looking down at me " I think it's cute" he said" What, this... This.. this.. thing...cute?" I asked in utter disbelieve and he finally let out his laughter.

I couldn't help but smile seeing him laugh like that, but I honestly didn't want this big bandage on my entire entire just because of a tiny cut which was on the tip of my finger." This will prevent it from getting infected" Gabriel said when he was done laughing "No, please, just put a little, not this... Please.." I pleaded putting my palms together in front of him

"No" Gabriel said, still smiling before he turned and climbed up the stairs. I complained continuously as I stamped my feet on the ground, I took another look at my finger.

**Later that evening, we all sat at the dinning eating, thankfully, it was my left hand that had the injury, so I could eat with my right hand. Abel sighted my bandaged hand. "What happened to your hand Liela?" He asked concerned making everyone's attention suddenly turn to me

"Jeez, what happened to you?" Mr Noah asked unknowingly adding to the tension, I immediately put my hand under the table away from sight,"She got a cut on her finger while helping me out in the kitchen" Mrs Fidelia announced"A small cut?" Mr Noah asked in disbelieve, of cause he had seen that my entire finger was bandaged.

" Oh, I thought bandaging the whole finger would be good, to avoid infection getting into it" Gabriel said holding back a smile, he seemed to be getting alot of joy from this. Mr Noah nodded in agreement " Oh yes, that's so thoughtful of you Gabriel" Mr Noah praised. I was shocked, I looked at Mr Noah, so he was in support of this?

I looked at Gabriel again with a glare, he winked at me with a taunting smile, I looked back at my food not wanting to look at him " I think it's really big" Abel said, and I looked back up

" That's exactly what I'm complaining about" I spoke seeing that someone was finally on my side, but I guess I was too quick" But it does look good on you" Abel added and my eyes widened . I seemed to be alone. Gabriel was totally enjoying this and I knew it. Mrs Fidelia patted my shoulder and everyone started eating again.

The weekend went by quickly and before we knew it, it was Monday again. Gabriel had changed my bandage but he didn't make it smaller, I had dramatically refused talking to him and he found it funny. So annoying.

I couldn't go to school with my hand bandaged like this, but no one agreed to listen to me no matter how many times I told them my finger was fine and I could go without a bandage.

Gabriel kept giving unreasonable logics on why my finger needs to remain bandaged and they all agreed with him.

That day when we got to school, we both attended maths class together , we sat close to each other but I didn't talk to him. The bell for lunch break was rang, I quickly left the class without waiting for Gabriel, I sat by myself at an empty table, soon other people started coming into the cafeteria.

The cafe was now filled up but the noise was louder today, everyone seemed to be talking about something I had no idea about. Theresa soon came over with her food tray and sat opposite me placing the tray on the table " Guess what?" Theresa said, a wide smile on her face "What?" I asked unable to guess

" The basketball match is coming up this Friday" she chirped. I didn't quite get it, she went on " The two basketball teams in the school would be playing against each other" she explained " Why do you look so happy about it?" I asked " Well.... It's a competition that has always took place in the school and it's always so fun, the exciting part is that Gabriel is playing..." Theresa spoke excitedly.

I looked at her, wondering why she'd be so excited just because Gabriel was playing " He always plays tho, but we're all always excited, he's the best player on the team. Harry would be playing too" she explained further" Shouldn't you be supporting your brother's team?" I asked with a bit of irritation in my tune, God, why was I getting upset.

Theresa served a spoonful of food and shoved it into her mouth, after chewing and swallowing she smiled again "Well.. good thing is, they're on the same team, so there isn't a problem at all" she said and continued eating with a big smile.

I had so many questions to ask her but I couldn't, why the hell was she happy? If they weren't in same team, would she have chosen Gabriel over her brother? Did she like Gabriel?. I sighed, I was happy they were on same team, I could support them both since one was my friend and the other was my cousin, no doubt I would have chosen Gabriel if I had to choose, but I was glad I didn't have to.

Chapter 15

"I'm so happy Liela, you'd attend right? So we could cheer for them" Theresa asked and I nodded without thinking about it. I turned to my food and started eating. I wasn't too comfortable knowing that she was so happy because of Gabriel. Why? I don't know, I just didn't like it. Well... I sighed again.

Later that day, after eating lunch at home, Abel went to his room to take a nap. Mrs Fidelia and Mr Noah were somewhere in the house, but out of sight, probably in their room or offices, I had no idea.

I sat on a couch alone in the living room thinking about the news Theresa gave me, I wanted to cheer for Gabriel.

I heard footsteps and looked to my left, it was Gabriel who climbed down the stairs and walked to me before sitting by my side "Are you okay?" He asked and I nodded "You don't look okay" he said. I sighed

Gabriel held my shoulders and made me face him "Is something bothering you?" He asked. I looked away from him " I still don't want to talk to you" I said stubbornly. Gabriel took my left hand and started unwrapping the bandage slowly

"Fine, I'm taking it off" I looked at him again smiling. He rolled his eyes at me "So childish" he commented and I frowned. "I'm not childish" I tried defending my self pouting my lips. He looked at me, his eyes falling to my lips, his hands stopped "Don't do that" he said almost whispering "What?" I asked looking at him innocently.

He looked away from my face and started unwrapping the bandage again " Forget it" he said dismissively.

He finished removing the bandage " Are you happy now?" He asked looking back at my face. I looked at my finger, turning in to the back and to the front again and folding my knuckles, a smile appearing on my lips.

I hugged him excitedly " Thank you, thank you, thank you" I screamed happily. I noticed he didn't hug me back, he was stiff under my hold, I quickly realized I probably wasn't supposed to hug him, I withdrew from him, he starred at me for a while before getting up " Sorry " I muttered " it's fine, I'll be in my room" he said and then he climbed up the stairs.

I was sad he left, why am I always so stupid?

We were having dinner that night, Gabriel finished eating and said goodnight to everyone, he got up heading for the stairs, I needed to talk to him, I quickly got up saying I had finished eating, they looked at me confused, but I hurried after Gabriel.

I got to him in the middle of the stairs, he looked at me" Gabriel" I started "What?" He asked "I heard about the basketball event and that you'd be playing" I said quickly, he only nodded in response. We kept walking until we got into the hallway, I held unto his forearm making him halt, he looked at me again

" I want to cheer for you" I said with a smile thinking it would make him happy " No" was his reply. My smile quickly fell ." You shouldn't attend the game, I don't want you there, so don't" Gabriel said, he looked a bit annoyed " But Gabriel..... Please, you're my cousin... I.." I was saying but he Interrupted

" Don't do that Liela, please, you don't need to attend the event, please do not push it, No, remains my answer" he said then walked into his room. I felt very disappointed, he didn't even want me to cheer for him, or even attend the match. Sigh, I walked to my room.

I sat alone in class, even when everyone had gone out. Harry walked in, his eyes landing on me and he walked to me

" Hey beautiful" he said smiling, I looked at him and smiled faintly " Hi" " Are you okay!" He asked and I nodded, he nodded as well" You'd attend the basketball match right?" He asked expectantly, i looked at him for a while

" I'm not sure" I finally spoke dropping my gaze sadly. " But why not? It would be so much fun. Okay, how about this, I'm inviting you" Harry said folding his arms against his chest. ' Wait! This is actually good, I could go and cheer for Harry instead and I'll still be able to watch Gabriel play, I could easily tell him, Harry invited me, so I didn't go for him, Good ' I thought and smiled at Harry before nodding

" Okay" I said " okay?" He asked with a wide smile wanting to be sure he heard me correctly " Yeah" I said nodding along. I and Harry talked on and on , I was happy. Harry was actually good company but I don't know, I wasn't too comfortable with him.

We got home after school and I decided not to tell Gabriel that I'd be attending, he might refuse, I'd just show up on that day and there... He wouldn't be able to refuse me anymore. ' Ha I'm so smart' I praised myself.

The day went by, we had dinner and all went to our rooms, the time was past 10pm, I couldn't sleep, I wanted to see Gabriel, he hadn't talked to me much today, and I wasn't comfortable, but it was already late, I had gone to check if he was in the living room but he wasn't, he probably decided to use the t.v in his room today or went to bed already. However I hoped he was still awake, but if he was, I couldn't just go there without a reason, the last time I got into his room, it didn't go so well, but that didn't stop me. I just wanted to be around him, I wanted him to see me, odd of me but I couldn't help the feeling. Just then, a light bulb clicked in my head. I knew I was smart. Okay not exactly but well there's no harm in flattering myself once in a while.

I picked up my phone and strolled out of my room, I walked to Gabriel's door and knocked softly but there was no reply, I knocked again, same silence, I lost hope, perhaps he was asleep already. I knocked one more time calling his name along in a whisper.

Still there was no reply, I sighed lowering my head in disappointment. The door suddenly cracked open, I quickly raised my head and my eyes met his, although I had to crane my head slightly " Hey" I said happily, but he wasn't smiling, he was frowning, he didn't look like he was sleeping, his hair was ruffled, I blinked.

My eyes slowly lowering from his face down , he was shirtless, this was the first time I'm seeing him completely shirtless and it was quite a sight.

Chapter 16

His chest was well defined, my eyes went down a bit more to look at his flat stomach decorated with abs, it was perfect, I looked at his arm and although I've seen them before, seeing him half naked made me want to touch them.. I wanted to look away but also didn't want to.

"Liela it's almost 11pm" Gabriel spoke distracting me from my thoughts, his voice deeper than usual, I looked at his face, his frown deepening" Did I disturb you?" I asked innocently, fighting to keep my eyes on his face. He sighed" What do you want?" He asked ignoring my question.

I dropped my gaze again, my eyes only just noticing his grey sweatpant that hung low on his waist showing the V-line that ran into his pants, leaving me trying to make out the end of the V in my head, I gulped silently, why was I thinking so much.

"Liela"I looked back to his face again." I.. I, I couldn't sleep..so... I was wondering.. if.. if I.. if ..you could keep me .. com..pany" I struggled with my words. His eyes softened. I couldn't help but think that Gabriel was avoiding me, but I wouldn't let that happen

"May..may..I..com..come. in?" I asked and his frown returned" Liela....I. I don't know about this" he said , he looked worried, I really didn't understand why" Please? I'm scared to be alone in my room" I pleaded although I lied about being scared alone in my room

" Fine, but. ..." He paused " Fine" he repeated and stepped away from the door so I could go in. I walked into the room, the lights were blue, making everything else in the room blue, and also making it difficult to see properly. Gabriel closed the door, he locked it but then paused and unlocked it again just letting it close. He turned to look at me, I just stood not knowing what to do.

I wanted to see him, but now that I was here, I was thinking if I shouldn't have. His eyes were fixed on me. He was still shirtless so I had to look at other things in the room to keep my eyes from roaming his body.

Gabriel walked to his bed and sat " So what do you want now?" He asked. " You.. you could go to bed, I just wanted someone around, go ahead with what you were doing" I said. He looked at me hesitantly but then laid down on the bed facing the ceiling, folded his right leg and put his right arm under his head. The position making his chest and abs more visible and attractive.

I turned away from him as I placed my phone on the table and started exploring the room touching almost everything I saw. I got to his closet, apart from the two doors that could be opened together at a time, there was another door which was on its own. I walked to it and attempted opening it but it immediately slammed shut.

I froze to the spot, Gabriel's palms rested on the door indicating he was the one who closed it back, I was shocked, his hands were by my sides caging me between his arms. I could feel him behind me. My back brushed against him lightly, the image of him being shirtless clouded my mind once again. Both our hands were still on the closet, he wasn't saying anything. I was so scared, he seemed angry, I knew I must have trespassed.

I slowly turned around to face him, craning my head to look at his face, I couldn't tell his facial expression, our position casting a darker shade of blue between us preventing me from seeing his face, but what I knew was.. he wasn't smiling.

" I'm.. I'm sorry" I muttered slowly lowering my gaze " Liela" he whispered, I looked back at his face " Do not ever open this door" he said seriously and I nodded. He went silent again still keeping me there, I lowered my gaze again. " I'm sorry" I apologized again and I heard him inhale deeply

We both fell silent, my fingers started playing with themselves out of nervousness, I couldn't look at his face, his marvelous looking abs captivating my eyes again. I looked down to the V-line that ran into pants leaving me to imagine, I honestly didn't know what was wrong with me, why was I staring?

" Liela..." I heard Gabriel mutter breathlessly and I quickly lifted my face to look at him, I realized he had moved even closer. I still couldn't see his face clearly

" Liela..... Stop looking at me like that" he spoke, his voice husky I blinked, afraid if he knew I was admiring him 'Heavenly Lord, why would I be admiring my cousin?' I thought

" Liela, you can't stay here... tonight" Gabriel whispered but I heard, I noticed his voice was becoming deeper with each passing second" Why?" I asked innocently. He starked down at me not saying a word and I bowed my head unable to hold his gaze.

" It's okay, I'll just leave then" I said sadly, he didn't reply so I took the opportunity and quickly bent down passing under his hands, I hurried to the door and opened it" Good night Gabriel" I said before hurrying away closing the door behind me.

Chapter 17

It was now Wednesday, I had no idea if Gabriel was angry with me, I was now always living with the fear of Gabriel being angry at me, I really didn't want to ever offend him, but I seemed to be doing that alot since the first day I moved in with them.

We had breakfast quietly and went to school, Gabriel didn't say any word to me, so I assumed he was angry. We had English class together, I sat at the back of the class alone and Gabriel walked over to me sitting by me , I looked at him but he didn't even spare me a glance. The lectures soon began but I couldn't concentrate, I bowed my head hating myself

" What's wrong?" I heard and quickly looked at Gabriel but his eyes were fixed on the teacher making me wonder if that was my imagination. I stared at the side profile of his face, soon he looked at me and our eyes met. I froze unable to look away, his eyes were so captivating, he bent his head to the side questioningly

" Liela" he whispered my name. But at the moment, my thoughts were else where, I liked the way he said my name, I blinked slowly, my eyes surveying his facial features. PERFECT was what I thought whenever I looked at him, my eyes dropping to his lips, pink and beautiful, probably...soft.... I looked back at his eyes but my gaze kept falling down to his lips.

I noticed he licked his lip, and I mimicked the action by licking my lip as well without even knowing it."Liela" he called again with more intensity and I was immediately brought back from wherever my mind was, my eyes widened at realization, I blinked

" What're you doing?" Gabriel asked, I looked at him, he wasn't smiling or frowning either, however there was a dark look in his eyes that I couldn't figure out "uh nothing" I quickly replied "Sorry" I added and looked away from him, this felt awkward for some reason.

I saw him throw his head backwards from the corner of my eye. I was tense throughout the class, he might no longer be mad at me but after my weird behavior just now, I have no idea what he thinks of me now.   Once it was time for lunch break and the bell rang, I immediately stood up in a hurry, with an attempt to get away from Gabriel but he held unto my wrist and stood up.   I looked at him, other students were going out of the class, some looked at us and murmured." Come with me" Gabriel spoke softly and walked out of the class, I hurriedly followed him.

We were now in the hallway, Gabriel was still walking ahead while I struggled to keep up with him, there were students in the hallway as well, we bent into another hallway, lined with doors at each sides "Where are we going?" I asked impatiently as I hurried to his side trying to match his pace. "To the cafe" he replied "oh" I murmured.

We both entered the cafeteria, many eyes starred at us, uneasiness settling in me. Why do they always stare when ever I'm with Gabriel

"Liela...Come over" I heard, i turned to my right and saw Theresa with two other girls at a table, I smiled but before I could take a

step, Gabriel grabbed my arm stopping me, I looked back at him '
What is up with him?' I thought

" Stay with me" he said. Although the words sounded very clear
and simple, I couldn't help but read other meanings to it   '
Ridiculous' I thought as I shook my head to get rid of the thoughts.
His grip on my arm remained firm, he led me to an empty table and
made me sit after pulling out the chair for me, I just stared at him.

Gabriel walked away from me to the food counters. I bowed my
head looking down at my laps. People were secretly watching us,
I wondered how Theresa would feel about me not going to her.
Surprisingly I didn't feel so bad, I knew I wasn't a good friend.

After a few minutes, Gabriel came back to me holding a tray of
food, he placed it on the table, I looked at him, it was just food
enough for one person, "Are you not eating?" I asked " Stop asking
questions, go ahead and eat" he ordered pushing the tray to my
side of the table while he sat opposite me

I was hesitant, I was scared I might mess up myself while eating
and I didn't want him to see that, I starred at the food.   " I'd
return the food if you don't want to eat" Gabriel said. I kept quiet.
Am I willing to go hungry or embarrass myself before Gabriel, I
eat with him at the dinning almost everyday but I was still scared
knowing he'll be watching me, I wasn't confident in myself at all.

It didn't take much time before I came to a conclusion " I'll.. I'll.
I'm not hungry" I lied looking down at my laps. Gabriel was silent,
I raised my head to look at him and my eyes met his, he didn't look
happy' Could he tell I was lying?' I thought.

I quickly got up and walked to his side slowly holding his hand "
I'm really not hungry" I forced a smile. He looked at his hand which
was still in my grasp and I immediately let go" Sorry" Gabriel stood

up and walked out of the cafeteria, I hurried after him ignoring the eyes watching us and murmuring

We ended up going to the library, we sat opposite each other, Gabriel held a book in his hand quietly flipping through the pages once in a while, I just sat there with a book but not actually reading. I kept stealing glances at his handsome figure' Okay, something was definitely wrong with me these days' I thought.

_______________________Please please please Comment

Do y'all think Liela is beginning to discover her own feelings and also what do you think Gabriel is up to?

Don't forget to vote & Comment

Chapter 18

Gabriel's Pov

It was finally Friday and I've been doing better at not thinking of Liela in an inappropriate way, she was innocent, infact anyone could tell her level of innocence by just looking at her. But her small slim and sexy figure was doing dangerous things to me.

Whenever I looked at her or thought of her it was never good.

I looked forward to the basketball match coming up, I did feel bad for asking Liela not to attend but I had my reasons because damn she was my biggest distraction. I would be lying if I said I ever concentrated on anything else when she was around.

Liela's Pov

The match would be starting in thirty minutes from now, I sat on my bed, Gabriel had left for the match already, I was scared, I didn't want him to get angry at me. I looked at the clock and it was 3:21pm. I sat up summoning enough courage, I'd go, I really wanted to see him play.

' I'm sure he would change his mind when he actually saw me there ' I told myself hoping I would be right, I got dressed in a mini white plaited skirt and a blue hoodie, with white Converse shoes. I stood in front of the mirror, I didn't know what to do with my hair. After thinking for a while, I just put it in a loosed ponytail.

I smiled , Mrs Fidelia got me a bunch of makeup,but I've never used them, I had no idea what most of them were even used for, I thought of trying it out but decided against it, I was running late already. My phone rang and I hurriedly picked it up. It was a text from Theresa.

Theresa: I'm outside your house, hurry up.

I looked myself in the mirror once again before stepping out of my room, no one else was home. I got out of the house and locked the door. Theresa looked beautiful, she wore leggings and a cropped pink top, her hair styled. We both took a cab and went to school. Immediately the car started driving, I tensed up all-over again, not too long we arrived.

We were a bit late, there were already alot of other students sitting on the bleachers and the game was about to start, we quietly got in and sat almost at the back. I saw Gabriel, his back facing me, his hair looked like he's ran his hands through it a few times.

From the corner of my eyes, I saw Theresa waving with a big smile on her face, tracing her line of view , I spotted Harry, he was already looking at me and I smiled,he looked handsome, I raised my hand to wave slightly and he also waved back with a happy smile, he looked really happy to see me, if only Gabriel would be happy to see me too.

Just as that thought came, Gabriel turned around and looked up at me, ' Oh no ' I said within as our eyes met. Now this is Harry's fault, he shouldn't have waved like that, I was tense. Gabriel frowned, he didn't look happy at all. A whistle was blown and the game started, the boys all started running around the field with the ball.

Gabriel didn't join the game immediately, his eyes still on me until one of the boys touched him, he managed to look away and joined the game, but took another glance at me. The game was going pretty fast, I really didn't understand what was going on, but people were screaming, I saw Gabriel with the ball bouncing it around, but then he looked at me and the ball was taken from him.

The other team dropped the ball into the net, once, twice. It looked like a boy was trying to talk to Gabriel for a sec but Gabriel seemed to have angrily ignored him walking away from him. The game continued and Gabriel's team was... Failing. Gabriel kept looking at me almost every time. Was it my fault? I heard Theresa scream supportively, I decided to join her and not think too much.

Soon Harry was with the ball, alot of people were chanting Harry's name in support including Theresa and I decided to join in, it didn't feel so good cheering for Harry but I just wanted to participate..." Harry. Harry.. Harry..." We kept cheering, my eyes met with Gabriel's again and I quickly looked away.

Harry was about dropping the ball into the net, but before it could enter, Gabriel hit the ball away. Disappointed screams sounded in the air. Harry glared at Gabriel, but Gabriel didn't even pay him any attention, instead he looked at me with a frown. Harry said something to Gabriel but I couldn't hear it, however I could tell it wasn't something nice from the gestures, and still Gabriel ignored walking away from Harry picking up the Hem of his shirt and using it to wipe off the sweat on his face.

I couldn't help but look at his abs...., He dropped the shirt back and again our eyes locked. He looked.. ' Sexy ' My eyes widened at my own thoughts and I quickly looked away from me, my face heated up. All of a sudden I heard the sound of a whistle and I shot my gaze up again. I looked at Theresa

" Is the game over? They failed?" I asked in a panick. She sighed " No, they're just on a break" Theresa said while giving me a bottle of water " Give it to Harry, I'll give mine to Gabriel" she said excitedly, her dull mood had gone to nowhere land. I felt jealous, weird. I looked at her bottle of water.

By the time we got down, there were already alot of girls holding bottles of water waiting to give out water to the players. Gabriel and Harry were walking towards us, I tried my best not to look at Gabriel, but his eyes were digging holes on my body.

Chapter 19

I stretched the bottle of water towards Harry when they were close enough but before Harry could even lift his hand to take it, Gabriel snatched it from my hand, his eyes not leaving my face, I looked down. Harry had no choice but to take Theresa's bottle of water.

I heard the sound of the cover of the bottle come off the body. I peaked through my lashes and watched Gabriel gulp down the water, and how he used the back of his palm in wiping sweat from his forehead. He gaze returned to me as he covered the bottle of water. " Goo... good game" I muttered frightened trying to reduce the tension .

Harry smiled and moved closer "Thank you Liela, we usually do way better than this, I don't know what's going on" he spoke giving Gabriel an angry look before looking back at me with a smile. I looked at Harry " I'm sure you can do it" I tried to encourage not even knowing what I was saying, and also making sure not to look at Gabriel's face.

" Oh wow, thank you, I'll definitely make sure to..." Harry trailed off as Gabriel suddenly grabbed my wrist pulling me away with him. Harry frowned as he watched us leave.

I knew this wasn't going to be good. I just followed him. He led me out of the game hall and into the boys locker room before he let go of my wrist. I dropped my gaze. "What are you doing here?" Gabriel asked going straight to the point." I.. wanted to come support you" I stuttered" For goodness sake Liela, I told you not to come here" he raised his voice" You should go home" he added much calmer.

I looked at him "But why? I'm already here" I argued" I don't want you here" Those words coming from him broke my heart, I could feel tears threatening to surface in my eyes" If you don't want me to support you, then it's fine, I won't, but Harry did invite me, so I'm here for him" I say, I saw his frown deepen.

" So you're saying you came here for Harry?" Gabriel asked. Honestly I didn't, I came because I have never been able to experience such an event but most especially because I wanted to see Gabriel play, I wanted to be a support to him.

" Answer me, Liela" Gabriel said raising his voice as he moved closer, I stepped backward in fear." I.. I'm here for Harry" I lied, even the words were difficult to say but I had to " Wow" Anger, that was anger I heard in his voice " Fine then, let's see how good your Harry is" he said emphasizing on Your Harry and it pained me. He turned around and walked away.

Soon I was back sitting by Theresa on the bleachers , the game was about to start again. Theresa kept asking what happened between I and Gabriel but I told her it was nothing, I know she didn't believe me, but at least she didn't bug me about it.

The whistle was blown and the boys started running around again. Everyone had started shouting all over. Gabriel was running around with the ball until he dropped it into the net and I almost became deaf with the amount of screams of joys, Theresa was so happy. I just sat there watching, my mood was sour.

I noticed a frown was stuck on Gabriel's face throughout the game. He seemed to be playing with anger not caring if he knocked people down. Harry dropped the ball in the net once and the rest was Gabriel, they won and everyone who sat on the bleachers stood up excitedly.

I sat not being able to feel the joy. Gabriel's team gathered around jubilating, but Gabriel angrily shoved them away from himself and stormed out of the hall, I quickly said my goodbye to Theresa and hurried after Gabriel. I felt guilty, everyone was confused but went on jubilating. I ran to the boy's dressing room and stood outside.

I waited for some time before Gabriel walked out all dressed on a black leather jacket, black trousers, black Snickers and an inner grey shirt, his hair looked wet. He walked past me like I didn't exist, I hurried after him and held unto his arm " Gabriel" I muttered. He stood and looked at me, his eyes flaming with anger, I slowly let go of his hand and he started walking again.

I followed him behind, it was already evening, the sun was going down quickly, we walked out of the school building and headed for the school's parking lot.Gabriel walked to a black bike, he probably came with it, I stood not knowing what to do as usual.' Was he going to leave me behind?' I thought. " Gabriel?" I called softly standing by him.

"I..., Don't be mad at me, please?" I pleaded, I was going to cry, I couldn't hold it anymore.Gabriel ignored me and picked up the helmet from the handle of the bike and then put it over my head buckling it under my chin, I looked at his face ' He wasn't leaving me' i was happy but still he wasn't talking to me " Gabriel" I tried again.

" I'm only bringing you along, so mom doesn't ask me about you" he spoke and sat on the bike positioning himself on it. I stood, I couldn't tell if he was lying or not " You, you don't have a helmet?" I asked. " Liela stop acting like you care about me" Gabriel yelled angrily as he stared at me, he looked like he's been tired of me a long time ago.

I felt hurt, I did care about him, I sniffled allowing a tear to run down my cheek "You're driving me insane Liela, so stop. Please" he said very calmly, almost like he didn't want me to hear it. " Get on" he ordered. I let the tears drop and wiped them off before climbing on the bike and sat. Immediately he started the time and moved, I wrapped my hands around his waist and leaned my body on him.

The bike stopped abruptly ' Did he want me not to touch him?' I thought and more tears kept pouring " I.. I.. I'll fall ... Off if I don't hold you" I muttered in-between sobs, I heard him suck in a breathe before restarting the bike and off we went into the highway, speeding past buildings.

I was scared I'd fall so I held on tighter, the wind drying my tears . Soon we got home and drove into the compound.

Chapter 20

Gabriel's Pov

Liela unwrapped her hands from around my waist and climbed down the bike allowing me to finally think straight, I got off the bike and started unbuckling the helmet from her head, she kept starring at my face, but I did my best to ignore it. She had been crying and although it hurt me, I was still angry, I was angry at myself for getting jealous.

I was angry she chose Harry over me, she looked happy when Harry held the ball but not once did she even smile when I scored. I removed the helmet from her head.   She was going to start crying again. I walked away from her and towards the door trying to avoid seeing her cry, and she hurried after me. I entered the house and she followed me.

Mom, dad and Abel were already eating at the dinning " Oh Gabriel, Liela, come join us" Mom said happily, but then she noticed Liela's face "Why is Liela crying?" She asked. I looked at Liela "How would I know" I asked " I'll be in my room" Liela spoke softly and ran upstairs sobbing. I sighed.

" Gabriel what's going on?" Dad asked" I don't know, I'll be upstairs" I said not allowing them to respond before going up the stairs. I felt stupid for making Liela cry, I got to my room and opened the door but couldn't take it anymore, I closed my door and walked to Liela's room.

I knocked but no reply, I could hear her crying inside, I knocked again, "Liela, open up" I pleaded. The door slowly opened revealing Liela, she had taken off her hoodie, she was now on a cropped singlet, exposing her flat belly and belly button. Her eyes slightly red, tears on her cheeks. I stepped into the room closing the door behind me.

" Gabriel, I'm sorry, please don't be mad at me... I...." She tried to talk as she cried. I pulled her into my arms hugging her and placed her head on my chest "Shhh it's okay" I tried to comfort her, I wasn't good at it as I've never comforted anyone cause I never saw a reason to.   She slowly wrapped her arms around my torso and cried into my chest, I tapped her back softly

" I just wanted to attend, I've never gone to such an event before, I went there because I wanted to see you play Gabriel, please don't be mad at me..... Please...." She cried and i withdrew from her cupping her face in my hands as I brought my face lower bending my back slightly

" Don't cry Liela, it isn't your fault, I'm sorry, I didn't mean to upset you, I completely understand and I'm sorry for making you cry" I spoke softly while using my thumb in wiping her tears, I couldn't believe I was apologizing to a girl, I've always been proud, God! She was affecting me in many ways.

I starred down at her,i tried not to look at her lips but it was difficult, I held her face in my hands, her lips were a sharp pink, I swallowed down. I wanted to kiss her, I wanted to taste her lips more than anything at that moment. Just one kiss wouldn't hurt right? But I knew kissing her would make alot of things go wrong and I might never be able to stop. My eyes running over her face, I had to distract myself from kissing her.

"Liela, I can't concentrate, I can't concentrate on anything when you're around" I confessed breathlessly. Her eyes searched my face, she was confused " God, I can't think straight" I said again and pulled her into a tight hug as I dipped my face into the crook of her neck. I inhaled deeply,she smelt good, really good. She slowly clutched my Jacket, I grabbed her waist trying to get closer to her, every nerve in me was now aware of our closeness.

" Liela..., you smell good" I murmured into her neck and she shivered slightly. I fought the urge to plant kisses all over her neck. I felt her hand slowly sliding up my arm making me unable to think of anything else.   I wanted to lift her up and make her straddle me, put her on the table and kiss every inch of her body " Fuck" I cursed out loud.

It shocked Liela. My hands itched to move, I wanted to explore her thighs.... I stopped my thoughts, I hated the fact she was so young and innocent, I currently didn't even care that she was my cousin. " Liela, what the hell are you doing to me?" I whispered into her neck. I could feel her heart thump rapidly, she was trying to control her breathing and she was doing a bad job at it.

She breadth out of her mouth in an attempt to even her breathing but the sound she made while doing so fucked with my brain. I was clearly aware that she was also affected by me, it made me happy within.   I wanted her to moan my name, immediately the thought came in, I grabbed her closer, I couldn't help moving my lips, I placed a deep wet kiss on her neck and she ached her back pressing her body further into mine

" Uh... Gabe..." She tried to speak " Shhhh.." I stopped her "You're fucking toying with my head" I spoke again into her neck. She bent her head sideways, giving me more access to her neck " Gab.... Gabe.... Gabriel..... You ..." She stuttered unable to get her words together " Stop talking Liela, it's not going to end well" I warned, her voice was like fuel, it increased the fire in me, the sound of it played games with my mind, especially how she called my name.

I wasn't satisfied, I wanted to get rid of the jacket I was wearing and be completely pressed against her, I wanted her bare body against mine. God! Why did God make her my cousin. I was turning into a very bad sinner, not like I wasn't already.

Chapter 21

I had to leave, but I couldn't get myself to pull away, I had hardened more than I could even imagine and it was almost painful. However I was content with just having her in my arms like this, that was a lie I tried to make myself believe. I was pressed against her, I knew she was feeling my erection.

I wondered if she wasn't curious. One thing I knew was, Liela had always been deprived from any exposure, she never watched any adult movies or even read fictional romance like most girls do, she was pretty clueless about these things, however I was grateful she didn't ask what was poking her.

"Gabriel?" She muttered "Um?" I replied, my face still buried in her neck "Thank you for forgiving me" she said. I inhaled. I was never angry at her, I was just jealous "Have you forgiven me?" I asked. She immediately tried to withdraw, probably to look at my face but I stopped her pressing her tighter against myself

"Um, I wasn't angry at you" She spoke softly, her fingers slightly brushed the skin behind my neck making me suck in a breathe, I had to leave "You should go to bed now, it's late already" I said and just immediately, I noticed she wrapped her arms around my neck. 'Did she not want to?' I thought "Are you leaving?" She asked holding me tighter.

I heard the sadness in her voice. My heart skipped at the realization that she didn't want me to go " Fuck, Liela, I don't want to, but you need to go to bed" I tried to persuade her. "Tomorrow is a Saturday, please don't go" she pleaded tightening her grip on me even more. Fuck, she had no idea how much she was encouraging my demons.

The knowledge she wanted me made me want her more, I can't even explain how that was possible. God! I was ready to commit sins, I didn't mind if she was my cousin anymore . But I didn't want to taint her. I tried withdrawing from her but she held on tighter

" Don't go.., please stay" she kept pleading, she was so determined to keep me here, she held unto me like she wanted to get into my skin. Baby, that was what i wanted too only if it was possible. I didn't want her to go to bed sad, I hugged her again. I'll have to stay with her until she falls asleep before leaving.

I lifted her from the ground and she wrapped her legs around my waist tightly like I was going to disappear if she didn't. I walked us to her bed and tried putting her down but she wouldn't let go " Liela, I'm not leaving" I assured her, she slowly loosened her grip allowing me to lay her on the bed.

She starred at me, looking at her from underneath brought more dirty thoughts, I have decided to accept that I would never be able to think of anything proper when I'm with her. Although I wanted my jacket off, I decided to keep it on, it was a shield against feeling her direct skin. I laid on the edge of the bed, my shoes still on, one of my leg hanging off the bed.

I stretched my right arm out on the bed. I wanted her back in my arms, Liela seemed to also want that, she crawled into my arms hugging me and laying her head on my chest. I could feel her breadth evening as she quickly drifted off to sleep.

I waited until I was sure she was deeply asleep before slowly crawling out of her unbelievably tight grip, I placed a quick kiss on her forehead and then her cheek before heading back to my room.

God knew I wasn't happy with him. I had to sit in a cold shower for hours.

Liela's Pov

I woke up late, I stood up, I couldn't stop thinking about Gabriel's tight hug last night, my cheeks turned pink, I shyly held my cheeks in my hands. I stood in front of the mirror, my eyes were a bit swollen, but nothing too noticeable, I bit my bottom lip.

I missed his hold, I wanted him to hold me again. I felt things I haven't felt before last night, it was all so exciting, he had said alot but I couldn't remember most of it, and I just didn't understand some things, but he did apologise for making me cry.

I held my face. I brushed my teeth and took my bath, I wore a dress, put my hair in a bun and happily walked out of my room, I climbed down the stairs.   I saw Mrs Fidelia at the dinning operating her laptop, I strolled to her and she looked at me

"Good morning Liela" she smiled. I smiled back "Good morning ma" I greeted. "Come sit here" she said with a smile as she closed her laptop and put it aside. I walked to her and sat by her. "You look so happy this morning, did you and Gabriel..... get over what you two were about yesterday?" She asked. Just the thought made me blush.

"Okay?... I can see it's good between you two" she said. I dropped my gaze. "Um... Liela?" She Called calmly. I raised my face to meet her gaze " Did something happen?" Mrs Fidelia asked kindly.   My cheeks were flushed to a shade of pink. She arranged herself on her chair leaning a bit closer " How did you both settle?" She asked looking really interested.

I starred at her, she had been really nice, I wanted to be able to tell someone how I felt, I couldn't tell Theresa because I wasn't all that comfortable with her, but I was worried.   Gabriel was Mrs Fidelia's son and he was my cousin. I inhaled not seeing anything wrong in telling her.

" He apologized to me" I muttered innocently. She was silent as she starred at me , she looked like she was in deep thoughts for a second. She suddenly pulled her chair closer to mine and starred deep at me" Did he say anything special?" She emphasized on the word Special. I blinked.

Chapter 22

"It's okay, you can tell me" Mrs Fidelia said giving me a small smile." He said alot of things that I don't really understand and I don't remember some of it" I admitted."That's okay, I can help you, why don't you tell me what you remember" she urged.

I bit my lip nervously, I looked down at my hands that rested on my laps. " Okay, let's start..with... how he apologized, how did Gabriel apologize to you?" She asked in a calm tune. I looked at her again" He said. He was... Sorry..? He said, he was sorry for making me cry and...." I paused trying to remember "And that.....he....he..." I stopped again, " I can't remember " I told her softly.

She gave me an understanding smile making me ease up a little." Okay, did he do anything, like... You know.... Hold your hand..." She asked moving her head slowly" He...... hugged me.." I said scared." Oh wow, that's nice.... tell me more" she said smiling.

I felt so relieved " He hugged me very tightly, he told me I smelt good" I spoke a little more confidently." And you liked when he said that?" She teased and I tried holding back a smile, I bowed my head shyly" Was there anything else?" She asked.

I remembered he was using alot of curse words, I didn't know if I could tell her that" He was using curse words" I said softly biting my lip as I watched her facial expressions, her eyes widened but only for a second" How? What kind of curse words?" She asked

I couldn't speak,she probably figured it out "Was he using the F word....?" She drew her sentence and I nodded" How did he use it, was he like... Cursing on you" she asked. " No no no, he seemed to use it differently, I just can't explain it" I quickly defended Gabriel.

Mrs Fidelia took in a deep breath, swinging her hair backwards " That's interesting" she said. " Liela, I can't help you if you don't tell me what he actually said" she spoke calmly. I looked at her. She looked sincere, I was curious to know what Gabriel meant by a particular sentence

" He.. Gabriel.. he ..he did said something like..., He, he couldn't concentrate on anything when I'm around" I said feeling bad. I was confused as I watched a smile slowly form up on Mrs Fidelia's face. She looked like she understood what he meant, and I badly wanted to know, was I a distraction to him? Was it bad? I decided to tell her everything else.

" He also said, I mean, he told me, I don't know how to explain it" I was frustrated with myself." Calm down dear" Mrs Fidelia said, her smile not fading off, she placed her hand on my shoulder " Relax and tell me" she encouraged

" He asked me something like.. What was I doing to him?" I managed to say and then continued " I don't know if I hurt him or, or I might..." I was worried " Relax, relax" Mrs Fidelia laughed softly." You are fine my dear, is there anything else?" She asked.

I stared at her, thinking of what got my heart racing and I felt weird when Gabriel did that " He, Gabriel kissed my neck" I said and closed my eyes only to open them to see Mrs Fidelia looking at me with a smile that made me feel dumb.

" And did you feel anything..or no, let me put it in a better way, did you want him to go away or you wanted him to continue.... Like... Did you like it... Or not?" She asked watching me intensely, her eyes searching my face.

I could remember how I felt, my legs had felt weak, I would have been unable to stand on my feet if Gabriel wasn't holding me, then sensation I felt when he kissed me on the neck was foreign to me. I knew cousins weren't supposed to be like that but Gabriel didn't say it was wrong and I did like every moment of it.

I wanted to remain in his arms" I... I liked it" I confessed almost whispering but thankfully Mrs Fidelia heard it. She let out a breath like she was relieved to hear my reply" Then darling, you're just fine, and No, you're not doing anything bad to Gabriel, well... Maybe giving him a little trouble but I think he's cool with it and he can handle himself" Mrs Fidelia said

" Now here's the thing" she continued, her voice becoming more serious " Be careful with Gabriel, if you ever feel uncomfortable with anything he does, don't be afraid to tell him to stop, okay?" " Okay" I nodded, I got very relieved, but couldn't stop thinking about in what way I was giving Gabriel trouble.

Mrs Fidelia picked up her laptop and got up from her chair" I'm running late for a meeting dear, I'll see you later, if you ever want to talk about anything, I'm right here, okay?" She said with a smile and I nodded smiling back at her.

She walked over to the living room area, picked up her bag, put her laptop into it and hung the bag on her shoulder, she looked at me" And darling?" She called at me" Let this conversation be between us only okay? Don't let anyone else know, especially

Gabriel, alright?" "Alright" I replied" Take care sweetie" she smiled sweetly before walking out of the house.

I felt like weight had been taken off my shoulder now that I've told someone, but I was still a little worried.

Now that Mrs Fidelia had left, I realized I hadn't seen anyone else in the house. Where did they all go to? The house was silent. My stomach growled making me remember I had not eaten anything. I got up and walked into the kitchen.

Chapter 23

I sat alone in the living room, it was noon already and no one was home yet. Just as I stood up from the couch. The door opened and Gabriel walked in. I became still, starring at him. His hair was a complete mess, he looked sweaty.

He walked towards me " You're okay?" He asked and I quickly nodded not looking away from his face, he seemed to look better every single day." Liela, are you okay?" Gabriel asked again, worry etched on his face as he reached for my face. I cleared my throat slightly tearing my eyes from his face.

" I'm fine" I spoke. He breathed out in relief, I looked back at his face, I felt good knowing he worried about me, my thoughts going back to the previous night.   I wanted him to hold me again'Should I just ask him to hug me?' I thought but decided that wouldn't be good. I moved closer to him " I've been alone in the house, where did everyone go to?" I asked watching his face

" Oh" he exclaimed looking around the house until his gaze settled back on me " I went out with my friends, Abel attends piano lessons alot and sometimes just goes out with his friends so I'm not sure where he went, Dad traveled again. Mom...... Probably went to work" he said starring straight at me.

I dropped my gaze when I couldn't continue to hold the eye contact, I took another small step closer, I was now just inches apart from him. He was silent just watching me, I was nervous, very nervous. I didn't know if he'll get annoyed but I just really wanted him to hold me again" Gabriel?" I whispered while I starred at his chest "Yes?" He replied almost in a whisper too.

I slowly wrapped my hands around his body resting my head on his chest, he didn't hug me bad, I felt sad but didn't pull away " I was scared being home by myself" I admitted. My voice breaking slightly, I was going to break into tears, yes I was actually scared at home but Gabriel not returning my hug was what hurt me.

" I'm here now, you'll be fine" he said pealing my hands off him. He held my hands in his as he looked at me "Liela.....I'm all sweaty right now, let me take a quick shower, I'll be back" he explained. I looked up at his face" I won't take long, so wait here for me okay?" After saying that, he tapped my cheek lightly then turned and climbed upstairs.

I stood there suddenly feeling giddy 'Would he hug me when he gets back?" I thought smiling to myself. I walked to the couch and sat. I couldn't wait, what in the world was really wrong with me? I've never wanted anybody this close to me before. Well.... Not like anyone had tried to get close before now.

Minutes past, maybe ten.. I really couldn't tell, it did feel way longer than that to me. I heard steps from the stairs, I looked towards the stairs and saw Gabriel walking down the stairs shirtless, he was on a grey sweatpant, his hair damp and he was bare feet, his abs were just so... Attractive, making me want to touch them.

I looked back to his face and met his eyes, he flashed me the most charming smile I've ever seen. My face immediately heated up and I turned away from him.   I blinked rapidly 'What was that feeling?' I asked myself,I felt my stomach turn but not in a bad way, my heart beating faster.

While I was trying to get myself together, the space by me on the couch deeped in. I looked and saw Gabriel had already sat by me, I looked away quickly" Want to watch a movie?" He asked, his voice clear and calm" That would be nice" I replied immediately. I saw him smile from the corner of my eye" Are you that excited?" He asked getting up to go pick the remote and then coming back to sit by my side.

I didn't reply to that. "Liela?" The way he said my name made me feel tingles all over. I looked at him "What do you want to watch?" He asked. I shrugged ." Would you like to watch some romance?" He asked then looked at me with a smile.' Why was he smiling alot today?' I asked myself.

He looked away from me again. Soon a movie started playing on the screen. "Want some snacks?" He asked and I shook my head in a NO. I sat there trying to turn my attention from Gabriel to the movie.

Time flew by, the movie was actually interesting and I forgot Gabriel was even by me until the movie got to a point where a very muscular man and a girl were kissing and trying to take off each other's clothes. I quickly picked up the remote out of anxiety and turned off the television.

Everywhere suddenly became silent, I wasn't expecting that, I had never seen anything like that before. I have seen people kissing but not with that much aggressiveness and.... Why were they trying to have sex on screen., I was ignorant about alot of things but I've been taught about basic sex in school and that looked like it.

I looked at Gabriel to know if he saw it too but he was..... sleeping. His head was thrown backwards, his sitting posture was a bit slant, he was facing me slightly, seeing him in this state was different. He seemed so....So....I couldn't explain it. I shifted closer to him. I looked at his muscled arm, I used my index finger in poking it softly, it felt hard.

Curiosity taking the better of me, I ran my hand up his arm and down again. I liked the feeling of it, I knelt on the chair, so I could be able to look at his face. My eyes dropped to his lips, so..... Beautiful. I was a bit nervous but I won't always get this opportunity.

Chapter 24

I could study every feature of his face this close. I slowly drew an imaginary line with my index finger from his forehead, past his nose and to his lips. I stared at them. I blinked. I continued my trail down as I now sat on my legs. I trailed my finger from his lips down his chin and to his neck.

He looked so masculine, I used my finger in drawing a line on his neck and that instant, his Adams apple moved up and down. I took my hand back a little startled, studying it a bit more. I got even more curious.

I went closer resting my left hand on his arm and using my right hand in tracing his neck slowly continuously but it didn't move anymore. I decided to explore downward. I looked at his stomach which was decorated with strong muscles, I bent my head to the side as I admired them.

I placed both my hands on his stomach and glanced at his face but he didn't seem to be waking up. I started moving my hands slowly feeling the muscles, I used a finger in tracing all the lines and curves of his abs, I counted them.

I had never seen a boy so up close. He looked so attractive. His breathing was slow but it had been getting heavier. I wasn't worried tho as I didn't think too much about it, I was just focused on what I was doing, I wanted to be able to feel every muscle.

Gabriel's Pov

I was slowly drifting to sleep as I found the movie extra boring, however I said nothing since it seemed Liela found it interesting. I watched her for some time until my eyes got too heavy. I threw my head back and closed my eyes. I slept off but was still aware.

All of a sudden, I stopped hearing the sound of the television. I wanted to open my eyes but was too tired. Not long I sensed Liela move close to me. I waited, I wanted to know what she'd do. She poked my arm and soon her hands started caressing my arm slowly 'What in the world was she doing?' I thought, her touch felt good.

Her fingers soon started to draw a line down my face and she stopped at my lips ' God' She trailed downward to my neck, the moment her finger slid down my neck, I swallowed down in an attempt to not react to her touch but she pulled away that second.

I could feel her gaze. She continued not long after, her hand touching my arm and her fingers caressing my neck slowly 'Fuck! Did she know what she was doing?' My body was already reacting to it, although I kept trying to suppress the feeling. I felt her hands on my stomach, the contact awakening my goddamn nerves.

I waited, I anticipated her next move badly, and just then I felt her hands move slowly, her fingers drawing lined around my abs. ' God, was this her being curious? Because fuck hell, it was dangerous' I felt her hands moving upwards to my chest and she leaned in, I could now smell her and it was something I wanted to get more of.

I cursed within as her hands were slowly caressing my chest. Shit shit shit, I was loosing it, I didn't know how much longer I could pretend to be asleep. I wanted to pull her closer and make her sit on my lap so she could touch me while sitting on me then she'll know exactly how every one of her touch affected me.

I wanted to explore her body just like she was doing to mine and maybe a bit more...., I clenched my fists by my sides at that thought. My breathing had become reasonably heavy. I hoped she didn't notice that and so far, it seemed she didn't. Her fingers moved down so slowly drawing a straight line from between my chest down to my stomach, she didn't stop her trail there.

I felt my mother fucking dick harden more, her fingers went so low over my belly button and stopped at the waist band of my pants, it served as a hindrance. She wasn't moving, I knew I had hardened a great deal, I didn't want her to see my fucking dick upright. That might only spike her curiosity, and as much as I wanted her to touch me there, I knew she shouldn't.

I wasn't sure if she already saw the bulge, I quickly opened my eyes grabbing a pillow and putting it on my laps to cover my standing dick. She looked taken by shock as she moved backwards, her eyes wide open. She bit her lip making me want to kiss her

Fuck me, I shouldn't have acted so quickly. I stared at her, my breathing was heavy like I ran a thousand miles. I was now sure she noticed my erection, her eyes dropped to look at the pillow i used in covering my dick.' Fuck baby, you're making it swell even more when you look at it like that'

" Liela" I called. My voice raspy. She looked back at my face still in a shocked state. " Are you alright?" I asked. She stood up" I.... Gabriel...I... I'm feeling sleepy, I...I... want to go upstairs" she stuttered. I knew she was lieing but I nodded. Besides her presence was affecting me inappropriately. She didn't hesitate at all, she ran away.

I threw my head back. Damn. I missed her hands moving around my body, I wanted her to keep going. If only my fucker of a dick did not announce himself so soon.   With each passing day, my self control towards Liela was growing thinner, I've always been a play boy, I fucked around with girls and never got into any serious relationship, I always made it clear, it was always just about the sex.

I was never a good guy, I've always been generally aggressive, but with Liela, I seemed to be loosing it.

Chapter 25

Just thinking about Liela or seeing her turned me on, it scared me to an extent knowing I had no control over myself. I stopped bringing girls over when Liela moved in, and since then for some reason, I hadn't hooked up with any girl. I just wasn't interested.

I was almost irritated by the idea of being close to another girl. Even though I knew Liela was my cousin, it didn't stop me from feeling the way I did. I wasn't just sexually attracted to her, I was also becoming possessive of her, I hated that she even talked to Harry,I get jealous

I get pained when she's sad. I was fucking falling inlove with my cousin, that's if I wasn't already head over heels for her. Deep breathe. I was taking more cold showers than I could count and masturbating while thinking about her had become a routine. Although I couldn't do anything with her physically, I had violated her in my head countless times.

I remembered how she arched her back last night when I placed a kiss on her neck, I wanted that again, but this time, while she's underneath me, I shook my head.No. I needed a distraction from Liela,maybe if I invite a girl over,maybe fucking another girl would distract my mind from her.

Yes, that was probably what I needed to do. The thoughts of Liela still wouldn't stop tho. Her innocence wasn't helping matters too, the fact she was unknowingly getting attached to me. That was something I was well aware of, she was getting really attached.

She had hugged me earlier, I did like that but I knew to her it was an innocent need to be held but it wasn't an innocent action on my side, because nothing about my mind or needs were innocent. I had decided to suggest us watching a movie so she'd forget about the hug but look what happened instead, she decided to take a tour around my body.

Liela's PovDays turned into a week, my birthday was drawing close but all I could think about was Gabriel's constant movements. Once we got back from school, he goes out and comes back late, sometimes he leaves the house at night.

During weekends he's nowhere to be found. I noticed this started since the day I touched him, I knew I shouldn't have done that, I just didn't know what came over me.I was very sure he wasn't happy about that. Although he talked to me from time to time, I still had the feeling he was mad at me.

I want to confront him but I'm scared, should I just let it be? Each time we get closer to each other by an inch, we seem to drift apart again.

It was evening and again, Gabriel wasn't home. I wanted to know where he always went to but I knew I shouldn't interfere in his personal life even though I craved to be in his personal life, and that I couldn't even understand.

I sat in the living room all by myself scrolling through my phone. I received a text from Harry saying.

Harry Hello beautiful, how you doing?

I replied saying ' I'm okay' and he sent another text almost immediately.

Harry Are you home?

I just typed ' yeah'Not long, he sent a picture of himself. It was a selfie of him shirtless close to a swimming pool, water dripped from his hair and body. There were a few other people in the background minding their own business.

He had nice abs but I liked Gabriel's better, I couldn't help but compare them. While I was still looking at the picture, I heard the entrance door open. I raised my head from my phone and saw Gabriel who just entered the house. He closed the door behind him.

I slowly stood up placing my phone on the arm of the couch as I starred at Gabriel. He strolled towards me " Waiting for me?" He asked, no readable expression on his face. I nodded, he walked to me and only stopped when we were just inches apart forcing me to crane my head backwards to meet his gaze and I couldn't step back since the couch was right behind me.

" Missed me?" He asked almost whispering, his breath smelt slightly of .. I couldn't quite tell what the smell was (Author: the smell's alcohol). It wasn't heavy tho, it was just a faint smell.I nodded at his question, I did miss him. He remained silent starring at me until my phone beeped distracting us both.

We both looked at my phone, Harry had sent another text. My phone showing the picture of Harry and the new text under the picture. I felt instant embarrassment. Gabriel slowly picked up the phone looking at it.

My heart beat accelerated, I felt I've been caught doing something bad. I wondered what Harry sent this time. I watched as

Gabriel's eyebrows drew together in a frown." Send- me- yours" Gabriel read out loud. His eyes moving from the phone to look at me and I immediately dropped my gaze feeling guilty 'Why would Harry even send me a picture of himself shirtless?' I thought

I know he didn't mean any harm but him telling me to send him mine would read alot of other meanings to Gabriel which he might not have intended. Gabriel started typing in my phone as he spoke out loud. " Fuck. You" he said and tapped send. I realized he just sent that to Harry and I immediately tried taking the phone from him but he lifted it above his head, making me stand on my toes trying to reach for it.

" Gabriel please don't send that" I pleaded trying to reach for the phone "What? I already sent it" he said as he exchanged the phone to his other hand raising it higher " Please. Delete it" I pleaded " Why? You want to send him your nudes?" He asked angrily making me pause, my cheeks flushed slightly at the fact that Gabriel talked about me being naked.

Chapter 26

Gabriel lowered his hands making me stand on my feet again" Fine then, go ahead and delete it and then send him your nudes since you love him so much" Gabriel said angrily, shoving the phone into my hands and walked away heading up stairs. He seemed really angry again and i didn't want him mad at me, i quickly dropped the phone on the couch and hurried after him.

Gabriel walked into his room throwing the doors open angrily, I got there and quickly entered" Gabriel please don't be mad" I begged, my voice louder than I intended. Gabriel turned around facing me again and using his hands in closing the door behind me.

I moved back resting my back against the door while he stood in front of me, his left hand resting on the door by my head, he starred down at me intensely" What, don't you want to send your nudes to Harry anymore?" He asked leaning closer. I dropped my gaze nervously. Why was he repeatedly saying ' My nudes?'

"I...I didn't want to.... That isn't what he meant" I stuttered" You don't know Harry Liela, that was exactly what he was asking for, that's why he sent his first, it was a fucking open text" Gabriel said, his voice loud and filled with annoyance.

"You should go talk to your prince charming before he gets mad" He added. I slowly looked at him, he looked really angry. It hurt me knowing he was this angry at me " I'm sorry" I whispered, trying to hold back tears.

Gabriel didn't reply, the unusual smell (Alcohol) still lingered on him faintly. He slowly dropped his gaze looking down. My eyes immediately caught something on the side of his neck, it was a red stain. I kept examining the stain, my hand lifted and I touched it softly with my finger, causing Gabriel's eyes to snap back at me.

I withdrew my hand shocked at the speed at which he looked at me" What are you doing?" He asked. I softly cleared my throat, my eyes darting between his face and his neck until I summoned enough courage to lift my hand again to touch the red stain on his neck" You have....you have a..a red stain, here" I managed to say.

Gabriel lifted his hand to hold mine that was still on his neck and my eyes quickly settled on his face,he stared back at me, he looked like he was in thoughts for a second but then the look of realization appeared on his face" Oh, it's a girl who kissed me there" he said tilting his head sideways, his eyes on my face.

I glanced at his neck again realizing it was a lipstick stain, the lip shaped on his neck. I felt an unsettling feeling in my stomach, i slowly bowed my head, 'Why would he let a girl kiss him on his neck?' I thought."You want to be the one to kiss me there instead?" Gabriel asked and my eyes widened as I looked at him.

" No" I quickly defended my self. Honestly, I wish I could, but I wondered if he'll let me. I wanted to, I glanced at the stain on his neck again, I hated it, I wanted it off his neck.   Jealousy or was it envy? was building up inside of me. What was going on with me. I dropped my gaze not wanting to see the stain.

" Liela" Gabriel whispered my name but I refused to look at him" You're my cousin, I'm your cousin, we are related, we are... siblings, you know that right?" He asked . I nodded though confused at why he was bringing it up " Good, you can leave now" he said as he moved away from me walking towards his closet which was at the opposite end of the room.

I raised my face to watch him as he took off his jacket, he had red scratches on his shoulder blades and upper arm, I was sure more of those scratches were on his back hiding under the singlet, my eyes went wide. Gabriel threw the jacket on the bed and turned to face me again.

" Stop making me hate myself Liela. What? You also want to know how I got the marks?" He asked angrily. I was curious, I wanted to know but he looked really upset, I didn't understand why he was acting this was today.

I dropped my gaze" I'll tell you then" Gabriel spoke again walking back to me" I've been fucking alot of girls, I go out everyday just to fuck" he yelled angrily. What was he so angry about?" Or no. Maybe you wouldn't understand that. Ever heard of sex? Yes, I've been having sex with tons of girls just so I could fucking stop craving you" he spoke, every word with anger.

I looked down, this was what I was trying to avoid. It pained me to a great extent " Or don't you understand that too? I've been fucking around trying to fucking avoid you, but it's just so difficult because you keep getting into my face" he shouted.

'He hated me' I thought. A tear dropping from my eyes. I couldn't pick up every word he said but I knew he was angry and he used the word Fuck alot and he had been having sex with alot of girls.

" Liela" he said much calmer. He was now standing just about two feets away from me." Liela, I don't know what to do anymore, I'm confused, I don't know how to deal with any of this" he said. " I'm not a good guy Liela" he added. I raised my face to look at him " No. You're..." I tried to speak but he cut me off.

" For God's sake Liela, you don't know anything about me, I'm worse than Harry, you don't know him, you don't know me either, why the hell are you so innocent and clueless?" He yelled and I shrinked myself away wishing I could melt into the door. " I don't want you to be my cousin" he spoke quietly.

" Like for fucks sake, I hate it" he yelled again.

_______________________________Sorry for leaving y'all hanging again.

There have been some technical issues making it difficult for me to update the story.

But hope y'all like this chapter

Vote and Comment ✖

Chapter 27

His breathe was uneven, he was angry. I had never seen Gabriel like this before, I didn't know what to do. He just told me he hated me, I felt bad, I hated myself, how did I annoy him so much?

To an extent I also wished I wasn't his cousin, I wanted to be able to kiss him on the neck..or.. maybe he would be able to like me........? I sniffled.

"What do you want me to do Liela?" He asked suddenly. I looked at him and instead of anger, I saw helplessness in his features. Although I couldn't understand what was going on, I wanted to make him less angry. I stood glued to the ground not wanting to act out of my foolishness like I always do.

Gabriel picked up his jacket again and used it in wiping the lipstick stain from his neck although it didn't come off completely, he threw the jacket back on the bed before walking towards me. I pressed my back against the door frightened.

"I'm sorry" I found myself saying. He got to me and pulled me into his chest, dropping his face into my neck. I stiffened, I decided to remain still, not wanting to annoy him with the slightest movement.He inhaled deeply, pulling me even closer to him

"Baby" he muttered. I blinked wondering if I was the one he called that, my body slowly relaxing into him" I'm sorry for yelling at you, I'm sorry for everything I said" he said softly into my neck. I remained silent "Please don't get too attached to me, I won't always be reasonable" he said and I still kept quiet.

I wanted to make Gabriel happy somehow but I was scared to even move" God! Liela I'm sorry" he said, removing his face from my neck and starring directly at my face. I looked away, he used his index finger in bringing my face back to face him.

"Please say something" he pleaded "I..... I'm sorry" I managed to say, my voice breaking and I started crying. He held my head against his chest stroking my hair "Don't be sorry baby. I'm sorry. now please don't cry" he tried to comfort me.

"What should I do to apologise to you?" He asked. Immediately, the thought of asking him to allow me kiss him on his neck came to my mind but I shook my head getting rid of it. He kept stroking my hair and continuously apologizing.

I had left Gabriel's room the previous night when Mrs Fidelia came to call us for dinner. Since last night my mind had been disturbed. I couldn't forget all that Gabriel said. He had said it clearly that he hated that I was his cousin, which must have meant he hated me.

He also told me he had been hanging out with alot of girls and sleeping with them. That hurt me a great deal and I couldn't stop thinking about it, I didn't want him doing all that with other girls, but I was just his cousin. Who he hated.

The image of the lipstick stain on his neck was glued to my memory. It annoyed me. I wanted to kiss him on his neck for some reason, I wanted my lip there instead. The scratches on his body was another terrible image. Why would he let any girl do that to him. Did he like to get scratched by girls? Also he confirmed he's trying to avoid me.

Although he apologized and hugged me after everything, I still couldn't forget how angry he was, how he yelled at me. It reminded me of my stepmom who would make me kneel while she yelled at me about all my mistakes and how my mother was a prostitute and a home wrecker blah blah blah, all those didn't hurt me anymore. I had moved on from them.

Maybe if I wasn't Gabriel's cousin he would have liked me a little more? But would I have met him? I sighed.

I sat alone in the library at school, I came here so I could avoid Theresa, Harry and…. Gabriel, that's if he even cared about me. I just wanted to be able to think. I looked at the book in front of me and sighed, my mind only just going back to Harry, how was I going to explain I didn't send the text, I sighed again, surprised that I wasn't even that bothered about it.

" Boom" I heard all of a sudden from behind me. I quickly turned around startled. Theresa stood there with a wide smile. I stared at her blankly not even able to fake a smile. Seeing my reaction, she frowned, pulled out a chair by my side and sat on it. I looked away from her, now staring at the book in front of me again.

" You don't look happy, is everything alright?" Theresa asked "I'm fine" I said softly as I slowly closed the book in front of me." Why are you here then? All by yourself" she asked…" I'm just bored" I lied again.

Theresa was silent for a while before speaking again "Do you read novels?" She asked. I've read few novels. Mind you,, they were always educational novels teaching life lessons… Blah blah blah..

" Do you read romance novels?" She asked again gaining my interest" I haven't...." I didn't finish before she cut me off " I've read alot of them and I could give you if you want. I'm sure you'll like them" she said. I finally smiled.

Romance novels. I've never been able to lay my hands on any-thing of such. Throughout school, I managed in avoiding Harry, it didn't even seem like he wanted to talk to me. I sat in my room by myself. It was evening.

I have been avoiding Gabriel. I didn't want to talk to him, mostly because I didn't know what to say to him or how to even talk to him after all of that.

Chapter 28

He was my cousin and I was interfering way too much in his life. I shouldn't bother about the things he did, the people he hung out with or the girls.... But yet I did.

I got tired of being in my room, I went downstairs, while I was climbing down the stairs. I saw Gabriel in the living room area but he wasn't alone. I paused at the sight of the girl that was with him. She had blond slightly wavy hair, she wore an off shoulder skinny blouse and a mini skirt that seamed to be matching the blouse. The material of her outfit looked really thin.

She was on low heels. Her presence alone made my stomach sink painfully . She had her hands thrown over Gabriel's shoulders, I could only see her back. I started climbing down the stairs again not removing my eyes from them.

Gabriel looked away from her and looked at me, the girl turned her head to also look at me not removing her hands from Gabriel. The girl looked older than me and of cause she was.... beautiful, she had make-up on and all.

I got down the stairs and looked towards the dinning area. Mrs Fidelia was there 'How could they do what they were doing while Mrs Fidelia was just at the dinning here?' I I thought. Both Gabriel and the girl's eyes were on me " Liela darling" Mrs Fidelia called " Come join me here, would you?" She said with a wide smile.

I blinked, looking at the ground as I walked towards her trying not to look at Gabriel, but I could still feel his eyes on me. I got to Mrs Fidelia and pulled out the chair opposite hers. I sat down and looked at Gabriel again. His eyes were still on me. I looked at the girl and noticed her blouse had a V-neck exposing a good amount of her breasts.

She starred at Gabriel and glanced at me " Hey dear" Mrs Fidelia said snapping her fingers in front of me to get my attention and I looked at her" Pay attention here, not there, okay?" She said with a tender smile. I forced a smile.

I wanted to see what was going on with Gabriel and that girl but I didn't want to annoy Mrs Fidelia. She started talking with a very low voice, so only I could hear "You know since you came here, I've been so happy, I've always wanted a daughter..." She kept talking. It was obvious she was forcing the topics because she said alot of irrelevant and random stuffs.

" Umm.. can I go to my room?" I asked quietly. " Why? Because of them? No. Stay here" she smiled.   I wasn't comfortable here anymore. I could feel Gabriel's eyes on me from time to time. I didn't understand why Mrs Fidelia wouldn't let me leave

" Why?" I heard the girl's voice, she didn't sound happy. Mrs Fidelia looked so I quickly looked too. Gabriel grabbed her by the wrist and pulled her up the stairs. I looked back at Mrs Fidelia and she was already staring at me. I bowed my head.

The girl looked really beautiful. I couldn't stop my mind from thinking about what they went upstairs to do.

Gabriel's Pov

I dragged Hazel into my room before letting go of her. She was the only girl I had fucked more than thrice, to be exact I've fucked her five times and now she thinks she's something to me.

"What are you doing here for real?" I asked unable to keep the anger out of my tune. Hazel bent her head to the side folding her arms across her chest as she starred at me "Why all of a sudden? You didn't ask me what I was doing here until now" she spoke rudely.

She used to come over here just like alot of other girls before Liela's arrival. At first it was because I didn't want her to feel uncomfortable in the house, then it changed to because I didn't want her to have a bad impression about me and now it was because I have fallen in love and i didn't want anyone else.

Recently I had sex with Hazel thinking it would distract me from Liela but it didn't, did she think she's now allowed to come here again? "You don't just come to my house unannounced" I said trying not to be harsh. She raised an eyebrow at me and frowned.

She turned away from me slowly walking around the room, running her fingers along surfaces" You wouldn't let me if u had told you before coming. And I thought you had no problem with me here..... It's been a while, besides I just missed you" Hazel said as her hand slid across the closet door I had warned Liela never to open.

"Leave, I don't want you here" Her presence here made me highly uncomfortable. The look in Liela's eyes made me feel like I was cheating on her which wasn't likely since she was my cousin, not like I've ever worried if someone thought I was cheating on them or not.

" Why?" Hazel asked turning back to face me " Because of that bitch?" She spat angrily. I clenched my jaw at the word she used in referring to Liela.   I fought the need to bang her head against the wall." Who is she Gabriel? Your girlfriend?" She asked.

I didn't need to explain anything to Hazel but I wanted Liela's name clean " She's my cousin" I spoke my voice a bit louder. Hazel scoffed " oh really now? Your cousin. I saw the way you looked at her, I'm not stupid" she said raising her voice at me" Don't you fucking raise your voice in my house Hazel, you have no say in whatever I do, whether you believe it or not, she is my cousin" I spoke trying not to yell. God! I didn't want Liela in bad light.

Hazel strolled towards me angrily. Her acting like she was my girlfriend annoyed the shit out of me. She stopped three feet away from me " Oh so you're fucking your cousin?" She said, her voice low but coated in anger and disgust.

Chapter 29

My nose flared and my eyebrows pulled together. I immediately felt the urge to kill her, I wanted to kill her that instant, I stood still, both my hands in fists by my sides. "Gabriel is fucking his cousin" she yelled turning around like she was trying to announce it to the world. Then turned back to me.

"So that's why you shut us all out? You found a new pussy and got used to it. What? You like family pussy? How about you fuck your mother too" she yelled on top of her voice and I lost it at that. I grabbed her neck and slammed her back against the wall. Her hands flew to hold my hand that tightened on her neck with each second, trying to pry it away."Now you listen Hazel, I would only say this once, you'll shut your mouth and get out of my house this instant, you will not dare to ever talk about my mother or Liela like that again" I warned between gritted teeth.

"Are you trying to tell me I'm wrong or what? " Her voice low and choked."I don't need to prove anything to you" I said reducing my grip on her neck allowing her just a little bit of air before tightening it again

"You would leave now and not say a word to Liela, if you even take a single glance at her on your way out I'll know and you wouldn't like what would happen to you" "Is that a threat?" She asked" You and I know it's not Hazel. Don't play with me... I don't want to ever see you again" I pulled away from her.

She immediately squatted holding her neck as she coughed. " Stop the act and get the fuck out" I said as calmly as possible.She quickly stood up .   Her face red, the lines of my fingers were evident on her neck. She hurried out of the room. I could hear the sound of her heels going further away.

I breathed out and slowly sat on my bed. I starred at nothing in particular, my mind drifting back to the look in Liela's eyes earlier. I also knew mom was mad at me for some reason.

This wasn't the first time mom saw a girl come over. She was never pleased with my behavior but just accepted whatever I did. I ran my hand through my hair closing my eyes. I let myself fall backwards on the bed as I stared at the ceiling. I wasn't fucking Liela... Yet.

I stopped, I didn't like associating the word fuck with Liela. I wanted to maybe have sex with her No. Make Love to her, that sounded better.   But I guess God had decided to punish me this way. Deliberately making the only girl I feel things for to be my cousin.

Liela's Pov

A day had passed since that girl came over. She had hurried out of the house without even looking back. I'd be lieing if I said I wasn't curious to know what happened upstairs and why she left like that.

Although I felt relieved that she was now away from Gabriel, but of cause he could always meet her elsewhere. I kept avoiding Gabriel as much as I could, I spent most of the time in my room.

Theresa had given me a book tittled "Within his skin" On the cover was a man who sat on a horse with trees around. From his dressing I could tell it was a historical novel. The man on the cover looked really muscular, he had long black hair and he looked very attractive, he looked in his late twenties.

I looked down at the name of the author and the name was 'Tiana Emarak' I opened the book to the first chapter, the first sentence was "He has killed more than a thousand men, that even the emperor feared him. It was known to all that he was ruthless and cared for no one" I adjusted myself on the bed as I read on. Theresa said it was a romantic novel so I kept reading.

I woke up again at night, the novel was by my head on the bed. I sat up rubbing my eyes with the back of my palm. I slowly stood up. I walked out of my room, walking in the quiet hallway.

Gabriel opened his door and came out. I looked at him, he also stared at me without saying a word. I walked past him heading for the stairs" Liela" he called, I stood but didn't turn around" You didn't join us for dinner" he said. I remained silent. I could feel him coming closer to me.

"Liela, are you mad at me?" Gabriel asked. Yes, I was but wasn't sure if I had the right to be mad at him. Why would he allow a girl so close to him." No" I said, my voice coming out grumpy. I sighed.

He held me, turning me to face him " How can I make it up to you?" He asked. " I said I'm not angry" I said annoyed as I avoided looking at his face" That's a lie" he spoke.   I looked at his face, his eyebrows were pulled together forming a frown on his face. Why was he frowning? I thought I was the one supposed to be mad.

I pushed his hands off me as I stepped away from him "You didn't do anything to me so I'm not mad at you. You don't have to do anything" I spoke softly and Gabriel stepped closer to me again " Then...." He tried to speak but I quickly interrupted" Gabriel. I...I... don't want to talk to you" I muttered softly.

I tried walking past him in attempt to go back to my room, but I was pulled flush against Gabriel's chest. My eyes widening in shock.   My back against his chest as he wrapped his hands round my stomach, his face by the side of my face.

" Don't be like that. I'm sorry, I'm sorry for whatever it is you're mad about. I really can't live like this Liela" he spoke sounding desperate. Was I that important? Why wouldn't he just let me be angry?

Chapter 30

I tried to wiggle myself out of his embrace but he only tightened his grip on me and buried his face in my neck " Baby.." he whispered into my neck making goosebumps line my skin. I blinked. " I'm sorry" he continued.

" Gabriel . Let go" I said softly trying to unwrap his hands from around me. The effect of him speaking into my neck was one thing, and him calling me baby was another. I didn't like the way my body reacted to his tune either " Gabriel let go" I repeated louder" Are you this way because of Hazel?" He asked. I paused. Who is Hazel?

" Baby.. I didn't invite her over, she came of her own will and I sent her out. You wouldn't be seeing her anymore, infact no girl would be coming here ever again" he spoke softly in a reassuring tune into my neck and my body started to relax on its own accord.

" I... It's none of my business what you do or who you hang out with" I spoke, even though I knew that was a lie." Umm" Gabriel hummed . I tried to pull away again " Relax baby" Gabriel breath into my neck. I pressed my thighs together as I felt weird right at my core. I folded my lips."Gabriel.... I want to go to bed.." I said in an urgent tune.

" Do you forgive me?" He asked. I have but I feared if I told him, I wouldn't have his attention anymore. I remained still until he nuzzled his face in my neck causing me to shrink myself in his arms at the feeling.

" I can keep apologizing for an eternity, but I fear I won't survive that long if you don't forgive me now" Gabriel said. Although he sounded serious, I found it funny and accidentally let out a chuckle before I could stop it. I held my bottom lip between my teeth.

Gabriel slowly released me from his grip turning me around to face him, he held my waist again pulling me against him. I placed my hands on his chest to create a little space between us, although my lower body was still pressed against him. I looked up at him, his blue eyes were... darker and I felt I saw his pupils dilate.

" You like that?" He asked, I knew he was referring to what he said previously but I refused to reply. I frowned pouting my lip pretenciously, actually I felt happy within, I felt relieved that he didn't like that Hazel girl and he didn't hate me, infact I seemed pretty important to him.

Noticing his eyes were glued to my lip, I slowly stopped pouting my lips and started biting on it instead. Gabriel pulled me even closer, my hands on his chest not doing a really good job at keeping us apart.

His face now only inches from mine, I released my lip from between my teeth in attempt to bow my head but Gabriel's index finger and thumb held my chin back up. I stared at his face but his eyes seemed to be on my lips, his face drew closer and I closed my eyes. Was he going to kiss me? Why? Do cousins kiss? I pushed all of this to the back of my head, I wanted to be kissed by Gabriel, I wanted to feel his lips against mine. I've always wanted to know what kissing felt like.

Gabriel's nose brushed against mine lightly, his head tilted sideways as his lips made very light contact with mine but I didn't feel him kiss me, I felt his lips on the side of my lip instead making me wonder if I only imagined the light touch of his lips.

I unknowingly fisted a good amount of his shirt in my hands when his lips made contact with my jaw " Baby... Tell me what I have to do to make you forgive me" he whispered huskily into the side of my face. His lips placing small very light kisses on my jaw and upper neck.

I wanted to ask him to kiss me, but I knew that was stupid, he was still my cousin after all. I liked that he was my cousin but at the same time I hated it. His lips had started going lower, placing very light kisses on the crook of my neck and my shoulder. It made me a little frustrated, I wanted his lips to touch me properly.

This felt like a punishment, I gripped his shirt tighter, I was sure by the time I let go, the shirt would be slackened already but I didn't care. He was asking for my forgiveness and torturing me at the same time.

He suddenly stopped kissing my neck and I tugged on his shirt not wanting him to stop " Don't stop" I whispered vulnerably. At first Gabriel didn't move and I regretted saying that, I tried pulling away from him but I was surprised when I noticed I couldn't even move.

I looked at his face, he was now staring directly at me. His eyes looked so different, I felt naked with the way he stared at me" I was joking" I spoke quickly. I tried moving away again but his grip still unmoving " For real Gabriel, It was a joke" I lied again panicking within .

" I could do that for as long as you want if that would stop you from avoiding me" Gabriel said, his voice low. I blinked.   I could feel his lower body pressed against me, I fought the urge to look down, I felt wet in my panties. I had felt something like this before and it was also with Gabriel, he had been making me feel things I can't describe or talk about.

" Gabriel please let go... I've forgiven you" I pleaded " Liela" he said my name. I couldn't even think straight knowing there was something hard poking against my lower belly.

Chapter 31

" What's going on here?" Abel's voice rang startling me, I and Gabriel looked towards Abel's room and saw Abel standing outside in front of the door, he looked sleepy. I tried pulling away from Gabriel again but he still wouldn't let me" Go back to bed...." Gabriel was saying and I quickly interrupted

" I... We were... Talking, I'm hungry, something got into my eyes, so....so, Gabriel is trying to ...help me" I blabbered still struggling to get out of Gabriel's grip. " It's past 2am already" Abel said. His eyes on Gabriel's hand that was wrapped around my waist.

I hit Gabriel's hand and he finally let go. I hurried to Abel standing in front of him " I'm so sorry, did we disturb you?" I asked." No, I woke up and heard voices , so I just came to check" Abel said not looking at me but Gabriel, frowning at him.

I glanced at Gabriel who was behind me to see that he also had a frown on his face" Go back to bed, we won't disturb you anymore" I said" Liela, you should go to bed first" Abel said still frowning at Gabriel "Oh" I murmured

" Goo.. good night then" I said softly before turning around and heading for my room without looking at Gabriel. I did feel his eyes on me.. until I entered my room.

It was on a Thursday. Gabriel had been so close to me. We only seperated when i had a chemistry class and he didn't. However Harry was in the class and his eyes were trained on me throughout the entire lecture, making me uncomfortable.

He had not spoken to me ever since the text Gabriel sent him. Immediately the class was over, I packed my stuff and hurried out of the class with my backpack on my back.   I hurried down the hall and stood at a corner trying to pass time, so Harry would leave, but instead

" Hey" I heard, to my left was Harry, I looked at him shocked." W hat..what..what do you want?" I asked "Are we no longer friends?" He asked folding his arms" I..we are" I muttered" Look, I know you didn't send me that text. It has Gabriel written all over it" Harry said and I just stood starring at his face

" I'm also certain you didn't show him our texts willingly" he said but it sounded more like a question " I didn't" I quickly spoke.

He unfolded his arms and put his hands into his pockets" I thought you'd come explain it to me but instead, you decided to hide away from me, our friendship isn't that fragile is it?" He asked. I kept my gaze down.

" I was giving you time but I thought I might as well come to you since you wouldn't" he spoke calmly " So you're not angry?" I asked" At you? No. At Gabriel? I've never liked him" he said folding his arms again.

' Gabriel would say the same about you' I thought" So can you stop playing this hide and seek game with me?" Harry asked again and I nodded. He smiled "I... I... Gabriel must be wondering where I'm at" I said not waiting for him to reply before running away.

I exhaled and started walking again once I was out of his sight. I halted when I saw Gabriel and a boy standing at the end of the hallway talking. He looked at me and smiled.

I smiled back and he started walking towards me leaving the boy behind. "Are you hungry?" Gabriel asked once he got to me and I shook my head in the manner of NO. I wondered if he remembered that my birthday was the next day.

I stared up at him with a smile." Do you want something?" He asked. I shook my head again. His smile widened " Then what? A kiss?" He asked raising an eyebrow. My eyes widened and I dropped my gaze instantly.

That wasn't on my mind but now that he said it.... My thoughts were cut short when Gabriel stepped closer and held my face in his hands, he then placed a kiss on my forehead. He pulled his lips away but didn't let go of my face. I looked at his blue eyes as he starred at me.

I looked around and there were other students in the hallway, some stared at us, and others didn't seem to be paying attention, but there were also some who seemed to have nothing to do with their lives as they stood making it so obvious that they were watching.

I drew myself away from Gabriel taking two steps backwards. I felt like I was committing a sin in public. I looked up at Gabriel again realizing he was going to say something before I pulled away." I have some things to attend to for now, you stay out of trouble okay?" He said.

I thought he'd be mad at me for doing what I just did but he didn't seem angry. He still smiled at me before turning around. He walked back to the guy he was with, they had a short conversation but I couldn't hear them from the distance and then they walked away. I was happy. Gabriel seemed to be in a good mood recently and It made me happy too.

That evening, we all sat at the dinning having dinner. I didn't want to remind anyone about my birthday, they had been so nice to me already. I looked at Gabriel only to find that he was already looking at me. I looked back at my food.

"Are you okay?" He asked which of cause dragged the attention of everyone to us. "I.. Yes" I lied. "Why do you look like that then?" He asked further. I glanced at everyone else then back at Gabriel, I straightened my back.

"How? I'm really fine" I tried to sound more convincing. Gabriel only hummed, but didn't look away. I looked down at my food and started eating again. Everyone went back to their food..."What do you want for your birthday?" Gabriel suddenly asked. I raised my head to look at him.

Chapter 32

I raised my head to look at him, so he didn't forget? "Oh yes Liela, what do you want me to get you?" Mr Noah asked, I looked at him, I didn't know who to reply first. I knew what I wanted from Gabriel but I didn't know what I wanted from Mr Noah.

"Um, anything would be fine" I spoke softly, my gaze returning to Gabriel, I didn't really want anything from anyone else only if Gabriel would Grant my wish.

"Liela dear, is there anything you want specifically?" Mrs Fidelia asked. I couldn't think of anything, I just stared at her blankly" It's fine, it's fine, you don't have to stress about it" she said with a smile." Liela would be turning 17 tomorrow, wait..... Gabriel's birthday is just three months away" Abel announced.

"Liela, should I get you Chocolate?" Abel asked looking at me in excitement.' Was he that happy to get me chocolate?' I thought and smiled." How about surprising me?" I suggested and he quickly nodded happily.

I finally turned my attention back to Gabriel and my eyes widened realizing I ignored him the entire time. He didn't look angry tho " So.....!" Gabriel dragged reminding me he asked a question

" I want to spend the whole day with you tomorrow" I said nervously.   Everyone at the dinning looked at me " What? Ew, with Gabriel?" Abel said loudly. I bowed my head, my hopes dieing as Gabriel remained silent.

" I.... It's okay if..." I tried to speak" Shut up" Gabriel interrupted and I looked at him. He had started eating again. " Um that's actually a good wish, I mean, she must have gotten bored of only staying home and going to school, it would be nice if Gabriel showed her the city, don't you think?" Mrs Fidelia said

" Yes yes, that's good" Mr Noah nodded agreeing with the idea. I wasn't thinking about exploring the city but if that's the excuse that'll make Gabriel spend the day with me then I'd gladly use it, besides exploring the city would be great too.

I glanced at Gabriel who was only focused on his food, everyone soon went back to their food, so I resumed eating too.

I was in a deep sleep when I heard a knock on my door. I opened my eyes and another knock came, I looked at the clock and it was 12:03am, I sat up, too lazy to go open the door myself." The door is opened" I said sleepily hoping who ever was outside heard me.

The door slowly opened and Mrs Fidelia stepped in holding a cake in her hands, Abel followed behind and so as Mr Noah, then Gabriel finally followed and closed the door behind him.

I immediately started arranging my hair, I didn't want to look ugly in front of Gabriel. Once I was sure my hair wasn't hanging in different angles, I relaxed.

" Happy birthday to you   Happy birthday to you   Happy birthday, Happy birthday,   Happy birthday to you"

They sang as they walked closer to my bed. I could hear Mrs Fidelia's voice over every other person's, while Abel clapped. This felt like a dream, I had never before celebrated my birthday and now .... There were people who actually cared for me and took me as part of their family, what more could I ask for?

Mrs Fidelia stretched the cake towards me, there was a lit candle on the cake" Make a wish and blow" she spoke with a genuine kind smile. I smiled " I....wish..." I was saying" Ah.. no. You're supposed to close your eyes and don't say your wish out loud" Mr Noah said

My smile widened as I felt a little embarrassed, I looked at Gabriel, he stared at me with a smile and folded arms. " Go on..." Abel urged. I looked back at the cake in front of me and closed my eyes unable to get rid of the smile ' I wish that everyone here celebrating my birthday with me today, will remain happy for the rest of their lives and Gabriel grants my wish' I said within.

I opened my eyes and blew the candle but it didn't go off, I laughed softly and blew again before it went off and everyone clapped. I looked at Gabriel " Happy birthday Liela" Gabriel said, I don't know how it was possible that my smile could become wider than it already was but it happened.

" Happy birthday Liela" Abel screamed loudly. " Happy birthday" Mr Noah said almost immediately." Happy birthday dear" Mrs Fidelia said . I bit my lip trying to stop my smile from growing even bigger" Thank you.." I managed to say.

Mrs Fidelia handed the cake to Mr Noah and helped me out of the bed to my feet. I cut the cake with a knife Gabriel had been holding and fed everyone a bite each from the cake I was holding, I was the first to take a bite. When it was only Gabriel left, I walked to him , he guided my hand to his lips with his own hand giving me an intense stare.

His tongue licked my finger before he let go of my hand. I blushed and turned back to the others. Everyone started cutting from the cake and eating as it was now placed on the table. I stared at them and they all seemed happy. I looked at Gabriel, this felt unreal.

We had eaten half of the cake, I was now tired and I sat back on my bed. The time was now 12:47am. "Alright, you can go back to bed now okay?" Mrs Fidelia said and I nodded. Abel carried the rest of the cake and walked out." Sleep well, you have a long day tomorrow" Mr Noah said with a small nod and walked out.

" Okay, I'll leave now" Mrs Fidelia waved at me before going out. I looked at Gabriel as he slowly walked towards me.." Go ahead and lay down" he said softly. I folded my lips holding back a smile.

I lifted my legs from the floor and laid down still looking at him. He pulled the blanket up covering me with it, leaving only my head to view. "Thank you" I muttered. He didn't reply" Gabriel..... About what I asked for..." " Keep quiet and go back to bed" he cut me off and I nodded.

He turned around and walked to the door, he opened it then looked back at me" Don't bother preparing for school later today, we'll be taking the day off" he said with a smile he was obviously trying to hold back before walking out and closing the door behind him.

I was so excited, I closed my eyes trying to force myself to sleep. I just couldn't wait for the sun to rise.

Chapter 33

By the time I woke up, it was already 8:43am. I quickly got up and started preparing for the day, I brushed my teeth and took my bath. I wore a simple short floral dress, cute and not overdressed. I just let my hair down. I used a colour changing lipgloss that added more pink to my already pink lips. I also put mascara on my lashes and smiled in satisfaction.

I wore white Snickers as I couldn't decide what else to wear. I picked up my phone and stepped out of my room. The house was quiet ' Did Gabriel go to school forgetting it's my birthday' I thought.

I quickly stopped at his room door and knocked but there wasn't any reply, after knocking a few more times and still no reply, I stepped away from the door. Maybe he wasn't in his room.

I got to the stairs and looked towards the living room. Gabriel was sitting on a couch while he operated his phone.   A smile finally made it's way to my lips again. I started walking down the stairs, making sure my steps were loud.

I wanted him to look at me but to my disappointment, he didn't even glance in my direction. Either because he was too engrossed in his phone that he didn't hear me or he just didn't care to look.

I finally got down the stairs. I walked to Gabriel and stood in front of him, only then did he slowly lift his head from his phone, his eyes meeting mine." Good morning" I grinned. He smiled, his eyes moving from my face down my body. I got nervous, I stood still waiting for him to finish starring.

Gabriel's eyes returned to my face and he gave me a small smile " Morning, you slept well?" He asked as he stood up and I nodded while stepping back giving him some personal space. He put his phone into the back pocket of his trouser and picked up his leather jacket that was hung on the arm of the couch

He wore it while starring at me. This was the first time I ever put anything that had to do with makeup on my face. I was dying inside waiting for him to comment on it. Maybe tell me I'm beautiful or comment on my outfit, anything at all.

Gabriel picked up a bunch of keys from the couch " Let's go" he said and walked past me. My smile fell, I turned around and followed him behind. We got out of the house and Gabriel locked the door. He walked to a black car, I could tell it wasn't the one we usually took to school, this one was a bit smaller.

Gabriel opened the passenger seat and held it opened. " Get in" he said. "You... You're driving?" I asked. "Yes, get in" he said. "You can drive?" I asked again as I walked to him " Yes, get in" he repeated" Why does sir Marcus drive us to school then?" I asked as I got into the car and sat.

Gabriel closed the door and walked around the car to the other side, he opened the door and entered " He needs the job" he said as he started the car, he looked at me "Where do you wanna go?" He asked." I.. I don't know anywhere" I admitted." I'll take you to go eat breakfast first" he whispered but enough for me to hear and soon we drove out of the compound.

As we drove through the city, I took the opportunity to admire the view, I had gotten used to the view whenever we drove to school and back, but today, we went to a whole different direction. I could see both big and small businesses with their logos boldly drawn or written on the buildings.

People went by living their lives. I wondered what they did on a daily basis, I wondered if they were like me, what ran through their minds, where were they going? Or would they all pause when I couldn't see them and only start moving again when I'm around? If not.... How did they live their lives.

Did everyone have parents except me? Do they all really have birthdays.... Do they also..." Liela" I heard and I snapped my gaze towards Gabriel, he had a concerned look on his face." Are you alright?" He asked as he looked back at the road. I nodded" Yes" I said when I realized he didn't see me nod.

" I was asking what you'd like to eat" Gabriel said still looking at the road "I don't know......Just something light, I don't feel hungry" I said truthfully. "Okay" was all he said and kept driving.

We stopped in front of a restaurant, it looked beautiful. Almost everything inside was white, except for some plants here and there.... We sat at a table and Gabriel ordered salad for me and nothing for himself saying he already ate breakfast, I was grateful he didn't try to force me to eat actual food. I didn't feel like eating but I ate the salad anyway.

Immediately I was done eating, we left. We started driving again. Gabriel took me to alot of places, we went to an amusement park and it was my first time to ride on a rollercoaster, it was exciting but especially scary, but i knew I'd be fine since Gabriel was with me, we also went to a bookstore because I insisted on it while we were driving past one, but I didn't get any books. Gabriel didn't allow me to get any of the ones that caught my interest.

We went to a cinema and it was an amazing experience, I didn't really care about the movie, what I cared about was looking at Gabriel at intervals only to see that he was looking at me instead of the movie, and also the way the caressed my hand on the arm rest.

He also took me to a karaoke bar, I sang and sang until I got tired, Gabriel just sat watching me with a smile, he even clapped most times. We went to alot of other places and Gabriel made sure I ate countless times. Before we knew it, it was night. The time was currently 9:17pm.

We both walked out of a snacks stall by the road, I held a lollipop in my left hand" Are we going home now?" I asked as we walked towards the car. "No" Gabriel replied and I stood

He only turned to look at me when he got to the car" But it's late already" I complained. I was tired already. I enjoyed every moment but I felt exhausted, I wanted to rest" So you prefer standing there? Didn't you say you wanted to spend the whole day with me? The day isn't over yet" he said and I blinked.

Chapter 34

I thought about it. If we go home, Gabriel wouldn't be by me anymore, so.... I might as well just enjoy this while it lasts. I hurried to the car and stood in front of Gabriel, he starred down at me.

" Do you want to go home?" He asked, his voice low. I shook my head with a smile. Gabriel put his hand into his pocket and I followed the movement with my eyes, he brought out....I couldn't tell but I knew it was a jewelry.

He took my right hand in his and slowly put the...... bracelet around my wrist. I raised my face to take a look at his, only to find that he was already staring at me." Happy birthday Liela" he whispered. I blinked. I wasn't expecting any other gift from him.

I lifted my wrist up to take a better look at the bracelet. It was silver, had a few heart shapes around it. It looked so beautiful. I looked at him again. " It's beautiful.... Thank you" I said honestly." I'm glad you like it" he replied with an exhale.' Was he nervous?' I thought.

Did he think I wouldn't like it, aww, that was so cute. My smile widened visibly." What is it?" He asked." Nothing" I said shaking my head. I stared up at him for a while and without thinking. I lifted my self, standing on my toes and placed a light kiss on Gabriel's cheek.

I stood back on my feet as I watched his reaction. He was still , with widened eyes before slowly looking at me. I was sure my face was red by now. I quickly opened the car door and sat at the passenger seat, closing the door.

I hoped he wouldn't talk about what I just did. I sat there waiting for him to get in. Gabriel walked around the car and entered sitting himself on the drivers seat. After closing the door, he looked at me, I kept my eyes down while my hands rested on my laps.

Gabriel leaned closer pulling my seatbelt across my body but paused. " Don't play with me like that Liela. Might just make me feel you wouldn't mind" he whispered by my ear and then pressed his lip against my lower cheek, very close to my lip.

I froze in the spot. He finally belted me in and pulled away from me starting the car. I looked at him but he was now focused on driving.' What did he mean?' I asked myself within. Was he talking about kissing me? I doubted. I probably feel that way because I've been thinking about kissing him for some time now.

We drove to a..... club according to Gabriel, he got down from the car and walked around it while I unbelted myself, he opened the door for me and I came out avoiding his eyes. He held my hand, not my wrist, he actually held hands with me and walked in with me. There were two hefty men outside but I didn't even have the time to look at them.

I was flabbergasted when we entered. It was filled with people. Most of the girls were dressed in ways I could never imagine. They were almost naked, I looked away from them to take a look at Gabriel's face. He seemed to be looking for someone with his eyes.

There were different colors of lights. People were dancing and drinking......and.......kissing. I looked down at my feet.' Is this place for prostitution or what?' I thought. Why would Gabriel even bring me here?

He suddenly held my wrist and led me through some people to the bar area. There was a very Muscular man with bald head and no beards at all who stood there, he was obviously the bartender.

"Hey Gabriel, I haven't seen you for a while now" he say, his voice very deep" I've been busy" Gabriel replied

"Ah.. I see" the man nodded and his eyes finally landed on me" Who's this.... She looks..." He stopped trying to find a word "Cute" the man said and continued " Why bring such a....." He looked at Gabriel then back at me " She doesn't look like she belongs here" he said turning back to Gabriel.

Gabriel glanced at me " She's my cousin. I have to meet someone quickly, help me watch over her, I won't take long" he said and my eyes widened in realization that he was leaving me here." Liela, I'll be back, stay here for a few minutes please" he said and without letting me speak,he walked off...

" Welcome to... This. " He paused " welcome Angel, umm, don't accept to come here again next time" he grinned and I forced a smile " What do you want to drink?" He asked. I didn't have any money and I really didn't know if I wanted anything. However, the man who introduced himself as Millicent offered me a free drink.

It was a red wine and he said it wasn't alcoholic. It did taste sweet. I sat there waiting for Gabriel and after a while I saw him in the crowd talking to another guy while a girl clinged to his arm. I sat up straight. Wasn't he supposed to be spending my birthday with? Why was he now with another girl.

I stood up with an unknown determination. I strolled into the crowd. Once I got to where Gabriel was, I softly tapped on his back. He looked at me before turning to face me completely.

The girl's hold on him loosened as she let go of his arm, making me feel a little relaxed. " I told you to wait for me" Gabriel said " I'm tired of waiting over there, can't I be with you?" I asked. He just starred at me silently.

God! I wanted him to like me, not just as his cousin. I knew what I wanted was stupid and unreasonable but I couldn't stop craving extra attention from him. I don't know how it got to this but I just wanted to be someone he liked alot. I moved closer to him while I kept my gaze on his face.

His eyebrows were slightly drawn together. I placed my hands on his arms holding on to him softly, hoping he wouldn't reject me with what I'm about to do. I would cry forever if that happens.

I lifted my heels from the ground, now standing on my toes as I slowly lifted myself and placed my lip softly against his. I stayed for a bit and slowly withdrew, standing back on my feet. He didn't respond to the kiss, he definitely didn't like me, I should have thought about it properly before taking such an action. I looked at him and he wasn't giving away any expression.

His eyes running over my face " Liela" he spoke calmly. " I'm sorry" I said quickly. My eyed were about to tear up." I didn't know what I just did, I wasn't supposed... I..." I tried to explain. "Shut up" Gabriel said calmly and I looked at him.

Chapter 35

I hated myself. I didn't know if that was a real kiss or not, but he's going to think I'm weird and maybe get mad or tell Mrs Fidelia" Gabriel..." I cried. " Shut up" he repeated and grabbed my wrist pulling me along with him, out of the crowd. I just followed.

He led me into a hallway, the noise of the people in the club fading away. ' Where was he taking me?' I thought. I wanted to apologise but didn't want to annoy him any further. He opened a door along the hallway and led me in . It was a restroom.

He entered closing the door behind him and making sure to lock it. He turned to look at me. His eyes were a darker shade of blue. I leaned back against the counter as Gabriel walked closer.

"Liela"he called softly. I swallowed down, frightened as I pressed myself against the counter, wishing I could melt into it. Gabriel got so close as he towered over me. I looky up at his face.

" Liela. You have no idea, just how badly I want to kiss you right now" he said, his voice raspy and deep. My eyes widened. His left hand slowly lifted to hold my face as he brought his face closer to mine.

" Tell me to stop Liela, tell me we're cousins, tell me you don't want it, just. Fuck. Liela tell me you don't want me to kiss you" Gabriel said as he stared down at me. I just stared back at him in disbelieve. He wasn't mad at me? He wanted to kiss me too? " Please... Tell me not to" Gabriel pleaded, impatience evident in his tune.

Honestly, I had no intentions of telling him not to kiss me. I wanted this. I was more sure about this than I was about my grades. I wanted him to kiss me. However I remained silent.

" You want me to go ahead" Gabriel asked but it sounded more like a statement. Before I could even completely nod to his question. His lips were already against mine. My eyes widening in shock and then closed on its own.

He was slow only for the first second and then depeened the kiss, sucking on my lips hungrily. I felt his tongue slide across my lips making me part my lips and before I could figure out what was going on. His tongue was in my mouth. I couldn't keep up with how intense he kissed me but I tried to play along.

I loved every bit of how he kissed me. It was more than I expected of a kiss. Gabriel's hand held the back of my head in place as he kept kissing me like he wanted to explore the entirety of my mouth.

I began to run out of breath, I softly tugged on his shirt and thankfully he withdrew his lips and stared at me. I stared back, his eyes were so dark, I couldn't understand the hungry look he had on his face. Before I could blink. Gabriel lifted me and placed me to sit on the counter and he was between my legs.

Gabriel did not wait for another second before kissing me again. I felt a little sting on my lip but couldn't react as Gabriel sucked on my lips. Slowly his lips left mine and started placing hot wet kisses on my jaw and down my neck. I gasped at the feeling as I clutched unto him arching my back into him.

His hands grabbed my sides pulling me closer to him, while he continued assaulting my body with kisses. He kissed down to my shoulder and then to my chest, I threw my head backwards as a moan escaped my lips and I widened my eyes at the sound.

'What was I doing? What was going on?' I thought. "Gabriel" I called but my voice kept sounding like a moan. It was all Gabriel's fault. He wouldn't stop placing those open mouthed kisses on my body. 'What was going on with me?' this wasn't right, he shouldn't

"Gabriel" I called again and he slowly lifted his head to look at me. His lips looked slightly bigger than usual and hot pink, he looked gorgeous with his messy hair. I had forgotten what I had to say.

"Liela. stop moaning my name like that" Gabriel spoke breathlessly. I blinked, biting my lips and I noticed how his eyes dropped to my lips. I released my lip from my teeth as I shifted uncomfortably at the wetness in my panties.

What was going on with me? I felt a strong sensation at my core and it made me want Gabriel to continue and stop at the same time, I didn't know what to do.

Gabriel's Pov

I stared at Liela. Her lips were swollen as a result of my aggressive kissing, they were tempting and all I wanted was to resume kissing her all over again. I could see how her cheeks flushed. Her eyes were in a daze. She shifted on her seat.

I could tell she was turned on. If only she knew how hard my dick was in my pants. "Do you still want to spend the day with me or go home?" I asked and like I expected. She just stared at me not knowing which to pick.

"Do you know how beautiful you are today?" I asked. I have been holding back from saying this all day even though I knew Liela wanted me to compliment her. I held back knowing I might loose my senses if I spoke about it. She was cute, beautiful, gorgeous.

"When I saw you this morning Liela.." I paused watching her face, she was trying to hold back a smile " I almost couldn't stop staring. How can you look so beautiful, tempting me the entire time....." I didn't finish my sentence before

" Thank you" she said dropping her gaze shyly. I smiled." No... Baby. Don't thank me, I'm just stating facts" I said" Look at me" I demanded and she slowly lifted her head to look at me again.

" God.... I want to kiss you all over again. I want to keep kissing you until you can no longer feel your lips. How about that baby? Would you like that?" I asked. My breathing quickening again as I drew my face closer to hers. She was silent and I paused.

" Do you want to go home or stay with me all night?" I asked . She still kept quiet" Say something baby" I pressured loosing all of my patience. God! If she doesn't say anything. She wouldn't be leaving this place. I'd keep her here and fuck her senseless.

Fuck No. I wouldn't be fucking her. I'd be making love to her. Shit. She has to start talking. I was ready to go against every law. The one that says she's not an adult so can't have sex. Fuck that shit. She's been unknowingly teasing me for way too long.

Also the law that says cousins can't be together. Who even made that shitty law in the first place, because I'm about to not give a fuck about it

" Baby come on... Say something" I pleaded. " I..I.. think. Mom would be .. waiting for us" Liela stuttered. I stared at her." Forget about her. What do you want?" I asked hoping she'd choose staying with me.

Chapter 36

S he inhaled dropping her gaze." Let's go home" she spoke softly. I nodded slightly disappointed but relieved. I carried her down the counter and in no time, we were out of the club.

I noticed she was cold and gave her my jacket to wear. We got into the car and headed home. She avoided meeting my eyes throughout. I couldn't stop thinking about the previous events of the night. I knew I wouldn't be able to stop myself from getting closer to Liela anymore. At least not after this night.

It was almost 12am when we reached home. Liela quickly got out of the car and hurried into the house forgetting she had my jacket with her. I got down and strolled into the house. I climbed up the stairs realizing she had already gone into her room.

I wondered if she regretted what happened between us, I prayed she didn't. I don't know what I'd do if she starts thinking I took advantage of her. Shit! why didn't I think about all this before taking actions. Well..... Not like my mind was opened for thinking.

I walked into my room, immediately taking off my shirt and throwing it aside. I closed my eyes as I remembered Liela moaning and arching her back earlier. Fuck!

I wanted to know how she'd react when I stick my tongue in her pussy. Jeezz I needed to stop thinking. I ran my hand through my hair as I closed my eyes trying to picture the scene in my head.

I walked to my bed and sat as I started taking off my shoes. I kicked them away once I got them off. I paused, contemplating taking a shower, I was tired so I decided against it and laid down on the bed facing the ceiling. My left hand going under my head.

I really wanted to do more to Liela, I wanted to see her shocked expression when I fill her up with my dick. I wanted to hear how she'd moan my name, maybe beg me for more, and of cause, I'd be willing to. I closed my eyes as my dick hardened all over. I slowly put my hand into my trouser, planning to keep thinking about Liela while I ..

Knock knock

I looked towards the door. Who the fuck was that coming to disturb my...' Could it be Liela? Was she returning my jacket? Or.... She just missed me?' I thought as a small smile crept up my lips. Fuck. I'm crazy I know.

"Who's there?" I asked, loud enough for whoever was outside my door to hear." Gabriel, I need to talk to you?" It was mom's voice.' What the hell?' I thought as I retracted my hand from my trouser and sat up.

My thoughts running around. Was she coming to ask if Liela was okay?... Or.... How the day went? Or... Did she know what happened? ...... No, that wasn't possible. I got up as I walked towards the door." Gabriel? Are you there?" Mom's voice called and I opened the door.

She looked.... worried " What do you want mom? It's midnight and I'm tired, I need to get some sleep" I said even though I knew I had other plans other than sleeping." Gabriel. You'd get your sleep, but I need to talk to you first and it's really important" She said. Urgency in her tune.

I stared at her for a while " Fine" I gave in " Let's talk at the balcony" she said and walked away. I watched her leave wondering what was so important that we had to talk about right now that got her so worried.

I walked back into my room, wearing my shirt and walked out, telling myself to take a bath when I got back.

When I got to the balcony. Mom was pacing and only stopped when she saw me. A frown was etched on my forehead. The night was cold. I walked to her." What is it?" I asked. She let out a deep breath and held the railings while looking up the sky.

I stood by her with folded arms as the wind blew against my skin and hair. " You like Liela" She stated. I snapped my gaze towards her, she didn't look at me" You've caught feelings for Liela. Am I right?" She asked finally looking at me.

"What does that have to do with what you want to say?" I asked. She turned around completely to face me." It has everything to do with it Gabriel. So tell me. Have you fallen in love with Liela?" She asked seriously. I looked away from her. There was no need denying it

" I know you'd say I can't have feelings for her because she's my cousin. But..." " She's not your cousin" Mom interrupted starring straight at me. At first I paused processing what she just said. I turned to face her unfolding my arms.

" Mom? I don't understand what you just said" I said. I was confused. What did she mean by that?" I said Liela is not your cousin. She is not related to you in any way" Mom said.

My eyes widened. My ears were definitely deceiving me, I couldn't comprehend this...." Calm down and listen to me" mom said " Does Liela know this?" I asked and my suspicion was right. Mom shook her head indicating a No.

" Fuck mom. This isn't a fucking movie where you hide shit like this" I yelled." I said listen to me Gabriel" she yelled back." I called to tell you this because I noticed you liked her and she seems to feel same way for you" mom said.

Somewhere within me, I was happy, glad and joyful about this information but the current situation didn't allow me think much about it.

" Only I and your father knows this. Liela is the daughter of my brother's secretary and he is not her father. He fell Inlove with her but she refused to be with him because he was already married. She was later raped by unknown men and she got pregnant. She didn't want to abort the child. And because my brother, your late uncle liked her, he decided to take responsibility for her" she paused taking a deep breath.

" His wife thought he was cheating on her with Liela's mom, well he kinda was since he was trying to make moves with her, but they never had an affair. He always got into fights with her. After Liela was born. My brother and Liela's mother died together in a car accident. The car flew off a cliff and my brother's wife was the only one left to take care of Liela. While this was going on.... I wasn't aware" Mom narrated and stopped with a sad sigh.

By now I was calm. I folded my arms " So how did you know all this?" I asked.

Chapter 37

"My brother was a smart man. He scheduled a message to be sent to me at a particular date. By the time I received it, Liela was already leaving with my brother's wife. I was never on good terms with her so I stayed away because I had no claim on Liela. Until.... She died" Mom said. Her eyes now teary.

"I couldn't do anything while Liela was being maltreated in that Godforsaken woman's hands" Mom burst into tears. I moved closer to her and hugged her. I held her head against my chest

"It's alright mom, at least now, she's here with us and she's happy. I'm sure uncle and Liela's mom appreciates you and are happy wherever they are" I said. I just hope Liela's mom would be okay with me being with her daughter. I wasn't that good but she'd have to bear with me because I wasn't about to let go of Liela or let anyone else near her.

Now that I knew she wasn't my cousin. All the guilt in my chest flew away into thin air" You mustn't tell Liela about this" Mom said withdrawing from me while wiping her tears. I furrowed my eyebrows at that.

"Why?" I asked" I mean, let's give her some time. I know she needs to know, but not right now. At least maybe after you both graduate from highschool, then we could tell her, and Abel too.

Please Gabriel.. promise me you wouldn't tell her" Mom pleaded holding my hand.

I looked at her. Mom was precious. I couldn't insist on informing Liela even though I badly wanted to. I slowly used my hand in wiping her tears" Fine, I wouldn't tell her" I said. I didn't say this often, but I loved my mother. I wouldn't have wished for another even if I had the chance to.

We all sat at the dinning eating breakfast the next morning. I watched Liela quietly, she tried so hard to avoid meeting my eyes.

" How did spending the day with Gabriel go yesterday?" Abel asked and Liela immediately choked, she started coughing. I held back a smile. Mom gave her a cup of water and she quickly drank all of it, while mom rubbed on her back slowly

" Are you okay?" Mom asked her and she nodded rapidly. Liela glanced at me. She looked at Abel" It was fine" she replied to his question." You guys can chat after breakfast, let's eat. Liela choked already" Dad said. He didn't look happy this morning. No doubt it had to do with his business. I sighed and finally started eating.

Since it was a Saturday, we didn't need to go to school. I remained in my room. Abel had probably gone for his piano lessons. Mom went to work and dad ..... He was the last person I expected to be at home. I threw my phone aside on the bed as I sat up.

Liela had been avoiding me since morning. Although it annoyed me, I decided to give her some time to relax but not anymore. I walked out of my room. While walking down the stairs. I spotted her sitting on one of the couches, reading a book, she seemed pretty engrossed in it.

I stopped to admire her for a while, I didn't realize when a smile appeared on my lips. God didn't hate me after all, he knew exactly what he was doing. But damn, he really tried to fuck with me. Well.........I guess I deserved it. I started walking again.

Liela didn't notice my presence even when I was now standing in front of her. 'What was so interesting in the book?' I thought. I bent slightly so I could see, it was obviously a novel and she had read quite a good amount of it. I snatched the book from her lap and she jumped up instantly trying to take the book.

"Gabriel" she yelled my name. She seemed irritated by my action. Was the book that good? "What?" I asked trying to be more annoying. She calmed down "I was reading that" she whined. Arghh God! She's cute. I smiled "I know" I responded.

She opened her mouth to say something but closed it back. "That's why I took it, cause I want you to stop reading it" I said. "But I was about getting to the good part..." She murmured... I raised an eyebrow. I brought the book to my face in an attempt to look at the content of the book. Before I could look, Liela immediately tried to snatch it, but I quickly raised it up above my head where she couldn't reach.

"Gabriel, don't look at it... Please.." She pleaded. I starred at her, realizing the type of novel this was just by her reaction. "Are they fucking in the story?" I asked and I watched her cringe at the word 'Fuck'. I know she hated whenever I said it, but damn. It happened to be my favorite word.

I brought my face closer to her as I bent my back slightly." Do you like reading these type of novels?" I teased. She blinked and stepped backwards trying to get away from me. I straightened myself and frowned

"Who gave you this? Let me guess. Theresa". She dropped her gaze. "I.. I asked for it" she said. Obviously a fucking lie. "Yeah right"" I'm not saying you can't read this. I just don't like you being friends with that girl. She's bad influence and doesn't really take you as a friend" I tried to tell her but she frowned at me.

" You don't know anything. Will you give back my book?" She asked stretching her hand forward. " No" I stated. " And I'm sure Mom would love to see this" I said. I wasn't going to show it to mom though. I was just trying to scare her. Anything to spend more time with her.

Besides, not like mom would be mad about her reading this. I mean she's almost eighteen and is quite ignorant. " Fine then" she said. The lack of fear in her voice surprised me. She turned around and started going up the stairs.

" Where are you going to?" I asked. " To your room" she yelled. My eyes widened. 'Why was she going to my room?' I immediately followed her.

We entered my room and Liela quickly walked to my closet. She held the handle of the door I told her never to open' What in the world did she think she was doing?' I thought as I stood by the door. " I've been really curious about what's behind this door" she said raising her chin confidently.

I smiled and leaned against the wall as I watched her." If you don't give me back my book and promise not to say a word to mom. I'll open this door and see what you're hiding" She threatened.

Chapter 38

" Wow I'm so scared" I said sarcastically with a laugh. " Gabriel" she yelled in frustration. " I'm serious" she added." Okay, okay, but don't you think I could actually promise you now and then still tell Mom after removing whatever is hidden there?" I asked.

" You're a devil" She yelled angrily. I folded my arms " Are you just finding out?" I asked. God! I enjoyed annoying her." You're so difficult" She murmured but I heard. " Not when you turn me on" I replied as I tilted my head to the side with a smirk.

She furrowed her eyebrows at me. I pulled away from the wall knowing she didn't understand what I meant. Liela suddenly pulled the door open. But kept her gaze on me.

" I'm serious Gabriel. If you don't promise , I'll never believe anything you say again" she said.I smiled. "No. Go ahead and look" I said in a daring tune." Do you think I can't?" She asked. I chuckled. " Nope. It's just a matter of turning around" I said confidently.

Now that I knew she wasn't my cousin, I had no plans of hiding anything from her. Especially my feelings." Why aren't you looking Liela? Aren't you curious?" I asked. I actually wanted her to look now." If I look at it. It's a one time thing. I'll see it and I can't un-see it. Are you sure it's okay if I look?" She asked.

Her eyes pleading with me. She was curious to know what it was but didn't want to get me upset. I nodded with a smile. She quickly turned around and I watched how she froze.   She took a step closer. Looking at each and everyone of her picture that I've used in making a collage in the entire closet.On the door, the walls and everywhere.

I've been secretly taking pictures of her over the months she's been here. When I started craving to see her more but refused to admit my feelings to myself.

Sometimes she'd think I was operating my phone but I was taking pictures of her. I even started paying people to take pictures of her doing random things. It was creepy but I couldn't help it.

There were pictures of Liela randomly eating snacks while walking around in the house. There were others with her in school, eating in the cafeteria. In the hallway. In the fields. Sitting, standing, laughing.

There were others of her watching the television in the living room. Her eating alone at the dinning. Her, operating her phone and alot more. There was one very big picture of her. She was on a white camisole. She stood in the balcony. It was her side profile, but her face was turned to face the camera while the wind blew against her hair. She looked so beautiful.

I had taken that picture on a Sunday. I woke up and found Liela alone at the balcony watching the sunrise. She looked at me when I came into the balcony and I took a picture of her. I had denied taking a picture of her that day.

I stopped taking pictures of her secretly a while ago. When I decided to stop being a creep. Liela turned to look at me. She looked stunned and confused. "Gabriel... What. What is this?" She asked. "Your pictures" I stated like it was nothing. "But. Why do you have so many pictures of me here? When did these even happen? When did you take them?" She asked, not looking angry.

That made me relax a little because my mind had been thinking about the possibility of her getting mad. "That's a secret" I smiled trying to make her see that I mean no harm. She strolled towards me, holding back a smile. She stopped when she was right in front of me.

"So... You think I'm pretty?" She asked blinking. I burst into laughter unable to hold it back. She frowned. "Gabriel..." She whined. I finally stopped laughing and starred at her. "Yes" I said "Yes Liela. I find you so beautiful, anyone who doesn't think so is definitely blind" I added and she blushed hard.

She looked back at the pictures and looked at me again." I'm sorry for taking pictures of you without your permission. Forgive me... But please. Can I keep them?" I asked. She smiled." Only if you'll give me some. I don't own any picture of myself...and...." She paused now avoiding eye contact with me.

"You'll... Give me your pictures or let me take pictures of you with my phone" she pleaded. I smiled widely."I'll like that" I replied. She nodded in attempt to walk out of the room, but I held her back, my hands on her waist as I held her against myself.

I missed being so close to her. She looked up at me." I promise. Mom wouldn't hear about this book. Although she wouldn't get mad but I wouldn't tell her. I promise" I assured and gave her the book.

She nodded, still blushing. She took the book withdrawing from me and hurried out of the room. I smiled as I looked back to the closet. The doors hung open revealing Liela's pictures.

Liela's Pov

I liked Gabriel. I liked him so much. Days went by. Gabriel gave me his picture. Evil him. He gave me just one. However. He let me take pictures of him with my phone and I even took a few together with him.

I spent time looking at them. Gabriel didn't treat me like I wasn't important anymore. He never really treated me badly tho. It was probably me just seeking extra attention.

I didn't see any girls around him these days and he treated me like I was his.......... Girlfriend. Even in school. Which made people gossip about us. I try to avoid him in school knowing he didn't care about the people, but I did. Yet I never succeeded. I liked it tho.

It felt right to me. He would randomly corner me in places and kiss me on the lips. They were never just short kisses, it was always deep kisses. I knew if I didn't always stop him, he was ready to go on and on. I felt special around him.

I felt loved. The type of love I've always lacked all my life. Gabriel gave me more than enough and sometimes when he's so nice. I feel like crying.

Chapter 39

It was another day in school. Our exams were close by. I and Theresa sat at a table during lunch break. I knew Gabriel was right when he said Theresa wasn't my friend because she actually liked me, I knew it was because she wanted to use me in getting closer to Gabriel.

I didn't mind because I was desperate for a friend. But I've always been irritated by it.

She's been giving me weird attitude lately, it began when rumors started going around the school about how Gabriel and his cousin were being strangely close. Maybe she had realized that I wouldn't be able to help her in getting close to Gabriel.

Therefore, she had no use for me anymore. Most times she'd go sit with other girls, they'll talk and laugh while I sit all by myself.

I was surprised when she suddenly sat with me today. I slowly ate from my food while I also watched her . It felt awkward." You wouldn't talk to me?" Theresa asked" Um... I don't... Know what to say" I admitted.

She rolled her eyes at me, but i ignored it." You know my brother likes you right?" Theresa asked. When I raised my head to look at her, she folded her arms across her chest" I.... Don't understand" I was really confused." Harry. You know he likes you, stop acting like you don't know" Theresa spoke rudely.

I straightened my back. "Well... I know. I like him....." I was saying but she cut me off" Oh stop playing innocent Liela. You know exactly what I'm talking about" she raised her voice.

I did know what she was talking about but I was trying to avoid the topic. Harry had never personally told me he felt anything for me. He only asked to be my friend.   Although he made it obvious that he wanted us to be more than friends. However I felt nothing for him.

I felt uncomfortable whenever he talked to me. I've seen Harry acting same way he acts with me towards other girls. I knew Harry didn't actually like Love me. He was just like what Gabriel said he was. Just playing around for fun. I've seen him flirt with countless girls. I knew he did more than that though.

Even if he was righteous, I still wouldn't have liked him because I felt strongly for Gabriel.   I slowly covered my food as I stared at Theresa.

" Harry had never said he liked me and besides, I like someone else" I said. I mean, how can she be the one telling me Harry liked me. She was making it too obvious she wanted me out of the way so she could get closer to Gabriel.

Her eyes widened as she unfolded her arms. " Since when is that?" She asked, now curious. I didn't reply, I just sat there starring at her. Her face slowly changed to that if realization and then confusion. She leaned forward." Don't tell me it's Gabriel?" She asked in disbelief. I slowly nodded.

She leaned backward with wide eyes. " That's, that's, but you're cousins" she almost yelled. I packed my things and stood up." We're not" I said and walked out of the cafeteria.

I hurried into the library. There were only a few people inside. I walked to the shelves and stood between two shelves. I just wanted to be away from everyone at that moment, Including Gabriel. I stayed in the library just seated on the floor starring at the book shelf in front of me.

I felt regretful for telling Theresa about my feelings for Gabriel. ' Would she spread the news?' I thought. I was scared.   When I got bored. I picked up a book from the shelf and just scrolled through it, only reading sentences that caught my attention.

The school bell rang, I shot my head up in slight shock. ' School closed already? How long have I been here?' I asked myself as I quickly got up and kept the book back in the shelf. I slowly walked out of the library into the hallway. There were already students everywhere and others coming out of classes, creating a crowd in the hallway.

I bowed my head low trying to avoid any stares, just in case Theresa had spread the news but I noticed no one was starring tho. However I still kept my head low. I walked through the hallway, heading for the locker room so I could get my bag.

I collided into someone and staggered backward but I was immediately pulled back against the hard body. I looked up and it was Gabriel. I blinked. He had a deep frown on his face. I bowed my head not able to stop thinking about his hand that was wrapped around my waist holding me against him.

" Look at me" Gabriel demanded. I refused, there were people in the hallway and I knew they were secretly watching us. There were already rumors about us. Why was I suddenly so paranoid?.

I tried pulling away from Gabriel only for him to pull me closer. I looked up at him with a frown, he looked really angry. " Gabriel let go of me" I whispered in annoyance as I struggled to pull away. "Where have you been?" He asked. I paused and dropped my gaze to his chest.

" Not here Gabriel" I grumbled. I glanced at him only to see that his frown had deepened. Why was he so angry at me? " Leave me alone" I pushed against his chest and he let go. I looked at his face. He just stared at me. I could tell he was angry but I wasn't in a good mood either.

Why my mood became so sour, I had no idea. I walked past him. I finally got to the locker room and saw Harry" Hey beautiful" He smiled. I forced a smile in return. He walked up to me

" I haven't seen you in a while now, did I do something to offend you?" He asked leaning closer to me. I shook my head indicating a No. He used his hand in pushing my hair backward, a small smile playing on his lips.

Chapter 40

" You know? I get this feeling that you don't like me most of the time". Harry started. I remained silent. Before I could register what was going on, Harry pulled me into a hug. I froze at first, but decided to hug him back.

He would probably let go faster if I returned the hug. He did withdraw, and once he did, I walked to my locker and opened it while he followed me behind.

" You and Theresa don't hang out like you used to, is there a problem?" He asked.   I took out my bag from my locker and looked at Harry .

" She's your sister. I really don't know, maybe you should ask her" I said and attempted to leave. My eyes met with Gabriel who stood there with folded arms and a frown. I ignored him and walked away.

Gabriel's Pov

She walked past me like I wasn't there. I turned my gaze to Harry once she had left. Harry had a sly smile on his face and it annoyed the shit out of me.

" Agh... Gabriel. Seems you're not on good terms with miss beautiful" Harry said. My eyebrows drew together. Yes Liela was beautiful, but I hated him calling her that for some reason.

I exhaled" Harry" I started and he smiled raising an eyebrow " Long time, no convo" Harry responded.   I closed my eyes for a second. God this guy irritated me. I reopened my eyes

" This is a warning. I don't want to see you anywhere near Liela from now on" I went straight to the point. "Why? Are you her dad?" He asked.

I frowned at the mention of her dad. " This isn't basketball Harry. I'll beat the shit out of you" I warned in anger. " Trying to play big brother?" Harry asked as he leaned against a locker and folded his arms across his chest.

This guy had no idea how disgustingly annoying he was." Oh right! This isn't basketball, so true. At least I'll get to win against you in this one" Harry added as he leaned off the locker.

I Immediately grabbed his neck and slammed him back against the locker aggressively. He groaned in pain." God Harry! You have no idea what you're trying to do?" I spoke nonchalantly." You ain't the one who's gonna get married to her, so why even waste your time?" Harry said in anger.

I gritted my teeth" I would marry her" I stated . I watched Harry's eyes widen " What the hell?" He questioned in confusion. "Stay away from Liela for the last time" I warned before letting go of his neck and walked away.

I walked out of the school and saw that , our car was already parked in front of the school. I inhaled, knowing Liela was inside the car already. I walked towards the car and got in. Liela shifted away from me towards the other end. God! I'll kill somebody.

The car started and soon we were in the highway. I noticed Liela did not wear her seatbelt. I looked at her face " Liela" I called softly, but she ignored. I kept my eyes on her as she tried not to look at me.

I wondered what got her so angry. I moved closer to her, pulling the seatbelt from her other side, across her body as I made sure to be as close to her as possible. She was stiff. I belted her in before moving away from her. We remained quiet through out the drive home.

There was no one else in the house when we got there, I opened the door and walked in while Liela followed behind. I decided not to bother her since she didn't want to talk...

I was angry too, and jealous. She wouldn't talk to me but she let Harry touch her. Nevermind that. I still couldn't help but wonder where she went during lunch break and during classes. Harry and Theresa were also missing.

I searched for her almost everywhere but thought maybe they all went out together, but then. Theresa and Harry came back without Liela just before the closing bell was rang.

I climbed up the stairs trying not to think about all of this. She still thought we were cousins anyway. I listened to her footsteps as she also climbed up the stairs. Once I got to the top of the stairs, I walked towards my room.

I opened the door about walking in when I felt Liela's hands wrap around my stomach from behind. Her head rested on my back. My body immediately tensed up.'Was I imagining this?' I thought.

I remained quiet." Gabriel" I heard her voice break like she was going to cry. I immediately peeled her arms from around me and turned to face her, I cupped her face in my palms as I stared at her. Her eyes were teary.

" Liela" I said softly. I was mad worried. She pouted her lips "Tell me what happened" I urged." Why didn't you call me baby?" She grumbled as she dropped her gaze.

A smile quickly spread across my lips as I pulled her into a soft hug. She wrapped her hands around me. " I'm sorry baby" I apologized as I placed a quick kiss on her cheek." Gabriel I'm sorry for my behavior earlier... I went to the library and didn't know when the time flew by" she said.

" It's okay" I said relieved she wasn't with Harry. She slowly withdrew from me and stared up at me while i stared down at her." I know we're not cousins" she said.

I paused trying to understand what she said. My eyes slowly widened as I stared at her "What?" I muttered.

Epilogue

Liela's Pov

We all sat around the dinning table eating dinner. I looked at Gabriel who sat opposite me. He wasn't eating, he was just watching me instead. I blinked and looked away from him.

We both had agreed that I would tell everyone I already knew. I was scared, I wondered what their reaction would be. I looked at everyone, they looked okay and happy.

Would things change if they found out that I already knew I wasn't related to them? They've been really good to me and I didn't want to make things awkward, but I also knew telling them was the right thing to do.

I couldn't let them continue trying to hide it while I knew already. Besides, I didn't want them to disagree with me and Gabriel being together.

I took a deep breath, deciding to tell them once they were done eating. I tried to continue eating as well even though I had no appetite.

Mr Noah was the first to finish eating. He leaned backward resting his back against the chair's backrest. " Gabriel, why aren't you eating?" He asked. My eyes returned to Gabriel who still wouldn't get his eyes off me.

Mrs Fidelia and Abel also looked at him." Liela has something to say to everyone" Gabriel said. I dropped my gaze, but I saw Mrs Fidelia's eyes turn to me, she looked worried" My dear, is everything alright?" She asked.

I slowly raised my head . They had almost finished their food, so it wasn't that bad if I spoke now, besides Gabriel was impatient. I couldn't look at anyone.

" Do you want something?" Mr Noah asked and I quickly shook my head indicating a ' No' . I looked at Gabriel again and he gave me an encouraging nod. I dropped my eyes to the table.

" I....I.. I wanted to say that... I.. i want to let you know that..." I paused." Relax dear, don't be scared, take your time" Mrs Fidelia spoke softly as she rubbed my back soothingly. I felt like crying.

This woman was too nice to me. I tried to compose myself " I know I'm not related to you all" I quickly said. The silence afterward was loud. Not a single word or movement from anyone. Even Mrs Fidelia's hand on my back paused. I wanted to see their faces but was too scared to raise my face.

" I.. I'm not angry that it was hidden from me at all. I completely understand why and I truly appreciate all of your kindness towards me" I said. My voice breaking.

I slowly lifted my head. Mrs Fidelia looked at Gabriel and I quickly spoke before she'd blame Gabriel.

" I overheard everything the night you told Gabriel. I didn't mean to eavesdrop on your conversation, I promise. I just wanted to return Gabriel's Jacket that night, but couldn't find him in his room, so.. so... I went in search and I just happened to hear it" I explained as a tear threatened to drop down my cheek but I quickly wiped it off.

Abel cleared his throat, gaining everyone's attention" Mom, I've known this for quite a while, probably a week after Liela moved in. I was confused at why we didn't know we had a cousin all this while, and suddenly, she came to live with us. I heard you and dad's conversation about her" he paused and looked at Gabriel

" Gabriel seemed to be getting too close to Liela. I talked to him about it, but he'll only get angry and tell me to shut up. So I decided to act like I knew nothing" Abel added.

I could no longer hold back. Knowing that Abel knew I wasn't related to him but still treated me well made me feel so welcomed. Tears rolled down my cheeks and Mrs Fidelia held me closer putting my head on her shoulder

" It's okay. I'm so sorry we hid it from you" Mrs Fidelia said. The night was long. Mr Noah and Mrs Fidelia explained more about it to us. How everything happened in details. I felt relieved after understanding everything.